D1765698

WESTERN STORIES COLLECTION

FOR

MULTIPLE AUTHORS

Viktor Gjokaj

2019

ISBN: 9781693671319

TABLE OF CONTENTS

DESERT WATER --4

THE MAGNIFICENT SEVENTH -------------------------------10

THE SHINY GUN --16

FRONTIER CHRISTMAS-------------------------------------24

THAT NIGHT. A STORY OF THE OLD WEST -----------------35

THE SHOOTER- GHOST STORY OF THE OLD WEST---------46

THE SHOOTOUT---58

THE BLADE --60

THE STRANGER AND THE SALOON DOOR------------------66

DUSTY: A TALE OF THE OLD WEST --------------------------74

THE MAN WITH THE GUN. --------------------------------------81

AN EMPTY HOLSTER --85

BAD MEDICINE --100

SHERIFF, YOU KILLED MY BROTHER -----------------------114

COLORADO ---121

TUCK JACKSON AND THE CARSONS----------------------133

INTRODUCTION

There are so many reasons to love short stories; not least their ability to immerse us in new worlds in the time it takes to commute to work, or the common themes that weave through anthologies to create a thought-provoking whole. Here, we've collated our edit of the best short story collections. From spine-chilling tales and funny short stories to literary masterpieces, these are simply not to be missed.

Want to know the best way to stuff your vacation full of as many wonderful stories as possible? Spend your summer reading a few of the new short story collectionsi've picked out for you on this book. Each of these collections packs plenty of great stories.

I'm a huge proponent of short fiction, particularly for book-lovers who find that their daily lives get in the way of their reading time. A novel might take you weeks to finish, depending on how demanding your work schedule is, but a short story can be squeezed into the few minutes you have to read each day. You can experience a full narrative, from beginning to end, every day. Pretty snazzy, huh?

Short fiction also gives you the chance to get a taste for a new author you may have been wanting to a read for a long time.

Desert Water

By Eric Youmans

It was during the summer of 1974 when I motored down an arid stretch of road in northern Arizona. I was driving an old Buick LeSabre Convertible with leather interior, resisting the temptation to roll the top down. The feeling of wind in my hair, though refreshing, would not be worth being exposed to the blistering hot sun. The breeze coming through the open windows had to suffice.

As I gazed at the oncoming horizon, shimmering in the heat, my mind drifted to the phone call I got the day before. I was informed that my father died in a freak tractor accident at his home in Flagstaff. I hadn't seen the old man in a couple years but I kept in regular contact with him through phone calls. After I got the news, I packed a duffel bag and prepared to drive there from my Albuquerque residence to pay my final respects.

Even while I was daydreaming about the times I spent with my dad, I was aware that my gas tank was under a quarter full. Back then, you could drive a hundred miles in that region without seeing a town. Road signs were few and far between. I watched for them attentively as I drove, squinting because the heat of the day made them blurry when viewed from any distance greater than 10 feet. I wanted to find an exit sign, but like a desert oasis that turns out to be only a mirage, each sign I passed was a disappointment. Flagstaff: 138 Miles, read one. Beyond that, a sign informed me that I was Now Entering Navajo County.

I finally reached an exit, but as I pulled onto the far lane and coasted down to a stop sign, I noticed that I had another problem. My car was overheating. I needed to get some water in my radiator soon. The only nearby evidence of civilization was the road itself, paved with concrete by some long departed construction crew. I turned north at the end of the ramp. On both sides of me were vast stretches of desert. Only a few rocky formations and cactus plants broke up the monotony of flat, dry earth. I turned my attention to my dashboard, where the needle on my temperature gauge pegged into the red bar, warning of impending disaster. I drove ahead, trying to ignore the sinking feeling in my gut.

After a couple miles, I spotted some leafy trees up ahead. As I neared closer, the specks of greenery swelled into a dense tree line, at least a mile wide on the west side of the road. I pulled over to the shoulder and switched off the engine to let it cool by what I thought was the outer perimeter of a state forest. I figured that there would be a source of water in the vicinity, so I gathered some empty containers from my trunk and headed down a gentle slope toward the fertile area.

A few yards from the road, I found a tiny stream with a shallow rocky bed. No doubt this trickle of water would grow to a mighty river during the next deluge in these parts, where rain was infrequent but likely to cause flash floods when it did come. For the purpose of filling my water containers, this was going to do just fine.

Unbeknownst to me at the time, that small creek was the ribbon of life to local Indians upon whose reservation I was now trespassing.

I maneuvered around a thorny thicket and over slippery rocks, and knelt by the moving water. It glistened in the sunlight as I dipped my empty jug. The serenity of the scene was abruptly shattered by the creaky slam of a car door. I spun around and saw three figures exiting a pickup truck and moving down toward me. They made no attempt to be subtle.

Clad in dusty denim jeans and flannel shirts, the three men were unmistakably Native Americans. I sensed their hostility at the same moment that I glimpsed the weapon being carried by the shortest of them. It was a well worn but capable looking rifle, a 30/30 carbine probably used to hunt mule deer in the nearby hills. The leader was considerably taller than the rifle man, and though he appeared to be unarmed, his presence was more imposing. His pock marked face revealed nothing except a slight air of contempt. As he approached, he called out, "Hey!" and his two comrades moved to flank him on both sides.

This was before the days of wealthy tribal casinos and land grants. The tribes were still suffering under the white man's blanket of greed and prejudice. My people had wronged the Indians, and even though I was generations removed from the worst of those grievances, I felt that I might be tainted with some stain of ancestral guilt in the eyes of these men. I stood and raised my hand in a gesture of greeting; hoping not to become a target of their vengeance.

In a deep voice, the leader demanded, "What are you doing here?"

"I was just trying to get some water for my journey. I replied. My car started to overheat, and-"

"This is our water!" He interrupted. I swallowed hard and tried on a smile, but it felt sick. "You are trespassing on my reservation, mister. You do not belong here!"

Hopelessly outmatched in any physical contest, I decided to explain my situation and hope for the best. "I am deeply sorry for offending you, friend. I was driving to Flagstaff to attend my father's funeral.. I had some car trouble, and I'm running low on fuel, so I had to pull off the interstate. I thought that I might find a gas station off this exit, but there is none around here. If I had known that this was your stream, I would not have tried to take from it. I promise that I am no thief."

At some point during my rambling, the steeliness seemed to go out of the tall man. The short stocky one let the muzzle of his rifle drop toward the ground, and the erect postures of the men relaxed a tiny bit. A few moments later, he asked, "Your father died?"

"Yes he did. He was crushed by a tractor just two days ago."

"I am sorry to hear of your loss."

A long, awkward silence followed, while the leader appeared to be making a decision. Finally, he said "We have to watch out for people coming here. They come and hunt our game, catch our fish and litter our land with garbage. You understand?"

"Oh, yes." I said.

"If you want our water, you must pay. What do you have?"

I reached into my pocket and pulled out a crumpled $5 bill. "Here", I said, offering it to him. He took the money and tucked it into his pocket. "Okay," he said. "Fill your jugs and then leave here. Good luck."

With that, he and his two companions walked back up to their truck, leaving me standing by the stream. I breathed a heavy sigh of relief and bent down to the water to finish filling up my jugs, reflecting on the encounter.

Five minutes later, I was heading back to my Buick. The Indian's truck departed with a roar of its engine, its tires spinning up a plume of dust in its wake. To my surprise, there was a small gas can setting by the rear tire of my car. I picked it up and judged by the heft of it; there was at least two gallons of gasoline in there. I knew it must have been left by the Indians. I was touched that even after the historical injustices heaped upon them, they had enough kindness to help a white man in need. As I pondered the cultural values we shared, such as the desire to honor and remember our departed fathers, a single tear welled up in my eye.

The Magnificent Seventh

By Lisa McDonald

A Tequila sunrise cast an orange aura around the huge sillouette that stood resting both arms on either side of the saloon's duel swinging-doors. The hefty figure swaggered over to the bar and sat on the stool next to the vaquero that had just finished downing the last drop of Tequila in the glass.

"Gimmie a bottle of bourbon" escaped from the back of a dry throat as the big guy turned to look at the mexican who's coal black eyes locked with his. "Gimmie a bottle of tequila" the Vaquero snarled without breaking the stare.

You could almost hear the bartender's heart speed up as both men stared the other down in a heated battle of wills. They sat that way for quite a spell, tension filling the room as the bartender stood nervously drying and polishing the same shot glass over and over from the beads of sweat falling off his forehead...Admiring the vaqueros courage, "Names Jim" the big guy finally said lifting a dry, cracked hand from the Smith and Wesson that hung off his hip, and extended it in the usual formality..."Jose" came the reply as he too removed his hand from a holstered pistol and tightly gripped the hand of his rival, with a firm shake . They both sized one another up, each one secretly acknowledging the others brawn but remaining proud and self-assured, thoroughly convinced of their own brute skill.

Just as the bartenders heart began to slow itself down to a steady trot, The saloon doors swung open once again, as four of the roughest and toughest looking characters this side of Hell walked up and took their places at the bar, one at a time.

"Gimmie a bottle of bourbon" The first one scowled. "Gimmie a bottle of Tennessee" barked the second. "I'll have a bottle of scotch" Grunted the third. "A bottle of Tequila Gold right here" The fourth one glared, slamming a fist on the bar.

The big guy, sat up straight, flared his nostrils, flexing every bit of the brawn that covered his huge frame. He grabbed the bottle of bourbon and without wincing, downed the last half of the bottle. It flowed down easy as lemonade. Still holding-his-own, he placed the empty bottle back on the bar. The vaquero likewise lifted the bottle of tequila, snorted hard and without wincing, guzzled down the last half of the bottle and was currently savoring the worm. "Mmm, Sabe igual que el caramelo, like candy" He boasted.

But The Four ruffians sat in cold silence, staring straight ahead completely aloof.

"Uuuh...Don't believe I've seen you fellas around these parts b'fore...Da you gentlemen got a name?" The bartender asked The four, nervously patting and wiping the sweat from his dripping brow with the dish-towel.

But remaining obtuse, not a word or a breath escaped their lips.

"I don't know how it's done where you fellas come from, but round here, it's rude not to speak when spoken to!" The big guy said malignantly.

The first of The Four, rolled a look that could kill in the big guy's direction..."We got ONE name!" He said presumptuously "They call us.-"

"Eez that pose to mean somethin'?" The vaquero interrupted. "Huh? You think you somethin' cuz people call you only by one name?" He said, flicking and spitting out a piece of the hard shell lodged between his teeth that the worm left behind.

Before the vaquero finished speaking, the Roughneck had already returned to staring straight ahead, ignoring and refusing to acknowledge the mexican. Still, the muscles in his jaw bulged and flinched as he clinched down hard, grinding his teeth in a brief moment of restraint in his growing dis-like for the two men.

His three companions, eager to live up to their reputation, swallowed one last swig before slamming the bottles down and turning towards the big guy and the vaquero, hands at the draw and ready.

Jim stood up from the bar tall, proud and determined and faced The three.

Jose too, positioned his right hand at the draw above the Colt 45 hangin' off his waist, and his left behind him, gripping the Bowie knife hidden under his jacket.

The bartender grabbed a swig or two of his own when the first of the four decided that he had had about enough R&R and took his last shot of bourbon, lifted himself off the stool and joined his three companions. Jim steadily raised his arm to the draw behind Jose as the bartender squeezed into the crawl space under the counter, mumbling and babbling incoherently a rusty prayer that he once learned as a small boy and remembered only at that moment when his whole life began flashing before his eyes.

This was it. The moment of truth. There was no turning back now even if they wanted to. It was time to lay the cards on the table, see who were of mice, and who were of men.

12

...Suddenly the room grew dark. Something was blocking the light. Each one slowly took their eyes off of each other and turned towards the door.

In the doorway was a giant of a man, stood 6' 5" if he was a foot, weighed about 300 lbs. of sheer muscle. He dusted and shook himself off the remains of a days long spicy sandstorm before taking the last stool at the bar.

The first six did likewise, returning to their places at the bar, never once taking their eyes off the giant.

After a thick moment, the giant spoke...,"Is there a bartender around here?"

"Hhhere I am." He whimpered, raising himself up out from under the counter. "Wha-what can I get for you?"

"A muga beer with a shota whisky in it." The Giant answered.

The bartender hurried to fill his request, placing it carefully in front of the heaving mass of muscle.

The giant lifted the hefty mug to his chapped lips and drank it down in one gulp, slammed the mug down for a refill. "Another one" He motioned to the bartender. He did the same with the 2nd and 3rd and so on. All the while, 12 eyes at the bar remained firmly locked on his every move. He had had just about enough of the staring when he finally turned and said, "You got somethin' needs sayin'...say it!"

Not one of them bothered to speak their mind, or maybe they just didn't have the courage, so he turned back around, swallowed another beer and whisky, then quickly downed another six, one for each fella sitten at the bar. The giant was a bottomless pit, with no end to his thirst. They all watched intently as he drank'em all down, one after another just like it was fresh spring water on a hot day. It was around this time that the six began to realize exactly what they were up against. There was a fire in this giant, that neither hell nor high water could compete with. Still, everyone of'em but the giant felt they had somethin to prove.

The more belligerent of the "four", lazily cocked his head back and swallowed a shot of courage, slammed the bottle back down, lifted himself up off the stool and walked the long way around to the other side of the man, arrogantly leaned against the counter and tapped him on the shoulder. "You gotta name giant?"

He ignored the pesky fly leaning on the bar.

"HEY! I'm talkin' to you giant. Round here it's rude ta not speak when spoken to, so I'm goin to ask you one more time...You-got-a-name, giant?" He repeated a little slower as if the big man couldn't understand a full sentence.

The other five sensed an urge in their drawing arm to get ready, and figured it best to be prepared just in case. But the bartender now smiled and leaned confidently against the wall behind the bar, certain of the final outcome. There was not a question in his mind, which one of the seven was a "real man."

"Everybody's got a name" came the calm, cool reply.

"Yeah...and everybody's got a reputation too...You're a big fella" He said flicking the brim of the giant mans hat. "I'll bet you gotta big name and a big reputation to go with it too, don't ya?"

The giant went about his business, never saying a word in reply.

Not taking kindly to being ignored and wanting to flash his tail feathers, "Don't you wanna know who we are giant? You see my friends over here? He said, nodding his head in the direction of

14

the other three, "We four gotta reputation too? " He said, firmly nudging the big mans shoulder with his index finger, to no avail.

But the giant sat cool as a cucumber and waited for a refill.

"Ya know giant...? Outta the kindness of my heart, I'll tell you what I'm gonna do. I'm gonna do you a favor, and tell you just who me and my three companions are. They call us The.-"

"I know who you are" came the gritty reply. "I know who all of you are." He said, pouring down another beer and whisky before lifting his heavy frame from the bar stool, towering over the "pesky fly" as he flipped a gold coin to the bartender.

The bartender's smile grew wider.

No one said a word as the giant adjusted his hat atop his head then turned around to speak.

"The fella sittin' at the end of the bar over there's Jim Beam. The vaquero goes by the name Jose Cuervo, and you four gentlemen, they call-The Four Horsemen." He said, matter of factly in utter disinterest then headed for the door.

Each one now gorged with pride that the giant knew who they all were and was cognizant of their infamous reputations, now had their eyes glued to the giants back as never before, arrogantly watching as he left, when he suddenly stopped short and looked back over his shoulder one last time before exiting the saloon.

"But me" He said, pausing briefly, taking a final look at the six inflated egos..."Folks that KNOW me, call me The Boilermaker."

Then like the real man that he was, He tipped his hat and said, "Now you gentleman have yourselves a wonderful day." Then exited the saloon, leaving each and every last one of them thunderstruck, greatly relieved..., and still intact.

The shiny gun

By Kevin Hughes

Luke looked over at the tall man with the funny looking eyes. He had never seen eyes like that- kind of sliver, gold, ruby, and sapphire all mixed together. They didn't look real, more like metal or something shiny. Not as shiny as the man's gun though. It was the gun that drew Luke's attention.

That gun was silver. Pure silver. Polished silver. It looked mostly like a pistol, but even in its holster, you could tell it wasn't a Colt Thunderer, or Lightening, or even one of those new fangled Smith and Wesson's Model 3's. It wasn't a revolver of any type, because there wasn't any chamber for bullets in it. But it was definitely a gun.

By the looks of the holster, which was polished in its own way, but by use, not by a rag, that gun had been pulled out to do its dirty work many times. And that meant the man with the Metal Eyes was a Shooter. Since he was still alive, and upright, well…he must be a good Shooter.

Luke finished his drink and his assessment of the tall man at about the same time. Retreating to a table in the corner of the

Saloon with walls on both side- Luke settled in to see what the evening would bring. He was sure it would bring some excitement- he wanted to watch it, not be part of it. So he huddled in the corner, nursing his next drink. Waiting. He didn't have to wait long.

"Bartender! Drinks. Now."

The Bartender looked up. He knew that voice. A voice he was hoping he would never hear again. His eyes told him what his ears already knew; it was Black Bart. And his boys. Even Rattlers left those four alone. Not out of professional courtesy as some would have you believe; but like the rest of us, out of fear. The Bartender wasn't really a church going man, but he started praying as soon as he heard that voice. And one was a prayer of thanks that Mis Lucy had the night off from singing and serving. No way could anyone in this Saloon stop those boys from deciding to have a little fun. Fun that would leave Mis Lucy dead, pregnant, or crazy.

Out loud all he said was: "Coming up boys."

The man with the shiny pistol, metal eyes, and tall frame, never said a word. He never even looked up to size up the boys. Luke noticed. That scared Luke more than if the tall man had given a challenging look at Black Bart and his gang of toughs. Whoever this man was, wherever he was from, he was cut from granite, canyon wide shoulders with whip cord muscles that stood out like ropes on his arms, even when just relaxed.

17

The metal looking eyes added a strangeness to the man that Luke couldn't put a finger on. Like the man could calculate who you were, and what you were worth as a person - or an opponent, by just looking at you. A part of Luke's mind shivered. The part so primitive that it couldn't name fear, only feel it. Luke knew something was going to happen only now he was afraid he had made the wrong choice waiting to see it happen. The front of his brain was now shivering like the primitive part- both wishing they were somewhere else.

Black Bart and the boys got their drinks. Before they could take a drink though, Black Bart looked over and saw the Tall man with the metal eyes and the shiny gun. It only took a second for Black Bart to make his survey and come to a conclusion: Fresh Meat. Shiny guns were for tenderfeet, and Shooter wannabes. Black Bart's gun was as dark as his soul, the sixty one notches in the handle weren't all for killing inexperienced tenderfoot lackeys. No. Some of the best, quickest, fastest Shooters in the West, all went down under the smoking barrel of that coal black gun.

The only thing those sixty-one men had in common was that they were all dead. Tonight, Black Bart was pretty certain, that count would become sixty-two. But first, a little fun.

"Hey Stranger. Pick up your drink and join us in a toast. Hey, you hear me? Pick up your drink stranger."

You could hear the frustration in Black Bart's voice. Everyone could. Luke found that he wasn't alone anymore in the corner farthest away from the bar, the gang, and the man with the metal eyes. The Bartender had wisely left a bottle of whiskey on the bar in front of the gang, and had gone to the back room to get something. Anything.

"My name is not stranger."

Even Black Bart was caught by surprise. Mouths dropped open, jaws fell as slack jaws can. Eyes widened with surprise and delight. For a moment all anyone could do was to wonder if they heard what they thought they did. An Angel sing.

The tall man with the metal eyes and the shiny gun had a voice that was the prettiest thing they had ever heard. It wasn't feminine in any way, it wasn't fraught with male roughness, it was - well, the best word any of these rough frontier men could come up with was …pretty. Like honey, butter, and bacon, they wanted more of that voice.

It wasn't enough to stop Black Bart though. He had a hidden hatred for anything pretty, pure, or beautiful. Many women had found that out the hard way. Quite a few men too. Half the notches on that coal black gun came from the passing of just solid, men of good will, even kindness. So Black Bart killed them. No other reason was necessary. At least for Black Bart. The tall man had sealed his fate by using beauty against evil. He would make that pretty voice scream, beg, and cry before the night was over. He was sure of it.

"I said lift your drink and toast with us Stranger. I meant it. That shiny gun doesn't scare me. Nor does your pretty voice. "

"What do want me to toast to then?"

The Tall man with metal eyes, a rope hewn muscled body - and a shiny gun, still hadn't looked at Black Bart and his boys. His voice was as pretty as it was the first time, and hardened men found themselves hoping to hear it again. All except Black Bart. He hated the sound of the Tall man's voice. With its overtones of kindness, motherhood, safety, and truth. It was a voice a small child could believe, or a woman find safe and honest, or a man could trust. It made Black Bart mad.

"How about we toast to your quick death."

It wasn't a question. Not the way Black Bart said it. The Bartender decided to stay looking for something in the back room. Anything. Luke heard chair after chair scraping as men around him tried to actually back through a wall to get farther away from the scene at the bar. Black Bart's boys merely stepped to the left and right of Bart. Five deadly men. One lone man. Facing each other from only a few feet apart.

The tall man with the metallic eyes, shiny gun, cut wide and deep to ride the river with had turned to face the mean voiced man.

"I think not. "

The way that sound came out of the tall man's throat made everyone wonder why, just a moment ago they thought an Angel was singing. If anyone was singing now, it was death. You could hear it in his voice. Not an ounce of doubt in it anywhere.

Black Bart heard it too. So he didn't bother with his usual taunting. Or warning. He just slapped leather. Or tried. His hand hadn't even reached his holster, let alone his coal dark Colt- when he saw the shiny gun pointed at him. Part of him froze, for no one, no one human, could be that fast. Part of him was merely curious, for the shiny gun had no chambers. Just a barrel, and a trigger.

Black Bart's four tough gang members raised their hands as one. If Bart couldn't outdraw this stranger, they sure couldn't. They weren't cowards, but they weren't fools either. The tall man with the metallic eyes had already won, and they didn't want to lose their lives to prove it.

No one remembers how long they stood like that. Luke told folks it was for more than five minutes. Not a sound. Just a gun that didn't waver at all- and five men not even daring to breathe. Until Black Bart broke the spell.

"Well, you got your gun out. You gonna use it?"

He tried to sound tough, but he ended up sounding like one of his victims. His voice kind of plaintive and confused- every word leaking : "Just get it over with."

"Yes."

This time the tall man with the metallic eyes, wiry roped muscles, and shiny gun- sounded like God himself had issued an edict. A command. A statement.

Then the shiny gun went off. Rainbows shot out of the end of it in multi colored facets of light- like you see through a crystal or a Saloon window on a sunny day. The sound wasn't a bang, or bam, or boom, nor was there any smoke. A humming sound was all anyone heard. Then it was over.

No one saw the tall man put the gun back in its holster. No one saw him leave either. They were to busy looking at the five men on the ground. All five were crying. All five were holding their gun hand with their remaining hand. For all five of them were missing their gun hands. Gone. No fingers. No thumb. Just a stump remained. Black Bart was the first to get to his knees, tears streaming down his face in torrents.

His face a mask of regret, guilt, shame - and a thousand other emotions ranged across it too. Just like the other five men, his mind was showing him how wrong he had been, for how long, and what pain he caused for his victims: male, female, or child. It was almost to much to handle. He couldn't choke back the sobs, nor could he hide from the judgement his own mind was making about him.

Only then, did they hear the Angel Voice from the other side of the Saloon Door.

It was the most beautiful voice they had ever heard. This time it was colored with Hope.

"You fellas can grow your hands back, if you change your ways. You can't ever touch a gun again, or your other hand will go away too. Your one chance to get whole again, is to become a good person. A builder not a destroyer. If you build respect and not fear, your hand will grow back. The choice is yours."

No one saw the tall man with the metallic eyes and shiny gun again.

Luke saw Black Bart just about every Sunday. After all, Black Bart did marry Luke's sister Molly. But only after his hand grew back. It took three years. And no one spoke of what he was like before his hand grew back. No one called him Black Bart anymore either.

They called him: Lucky.

Frontier Christmas

By Kevin Hughes

She had her daughter pack up the bear claws. It took the last of her flour, and sugar. But she knew the men would be over the moon when they saw them, and drool when they ate them. It was worth it to her. She had her two boys hitch up the wagon. She had ham, bacon, and Buffalo steaks in the two giant pots, and beans…no cowboy would think a meal complete without beans. She also had ten winter apples for presents for the ten men. Her boys had finished with the tack, and hitting, so they call climbed on the wagon and off they went. She figured they would be somewhere within five miles of her place.

She figured dry gulch would be a likely place to start looking for the herd, and the men would be nearby. Dry gulch was a shallow natural gully, and would keep most of the wind off of the cattle, it wouldn't help much with the snow, but there wouldn't be many drifts. She had lived out here in the plains for nigh on seventeen years, and could read the land and weather as well as any Farmer, or Ranch hand, or Cowboy. So they would start looking for the men in Dry Gulch. If they weren't there, well, she figured they would be down a little farther by the river, maybe a mile or so away from the big bend. Ice and water made herding difficult, but if they had done a hard week before out on the trail, they might rest the cattle down by the river to get their fill.

As the wagon filled with food, the precious apples, and her two boys, three girls and herself bumped along the prairie she thought back to those same ten men, and how she met them all. It was two winters ago. The year after her husband had died from a broken leg. They didn't find his body until the Spring thaw. He had gotten the deer, but stepped in a gopher hole, and well, it was a hard way to go, dragging a broken leg, and 75 pounds of meat. She was proud of the fact that he had covered nigh on six miles, after breaking his leg. He was a good man. The meat was still wrapped in the skin of the deer and buffalo. When her husband realized he wasn't going to make it, his last act had been to bury the meat so the wolves wouldn't get it. They would eat him instead.

It was such a rough winter though, that the wolves didn't find his frozen body. His body was still froze through when Jack (her eldest) found it, along with the pebble sign her husband left to let them know there was a cache of meat nearby.

'Yep. Jeff was a man to ride the river with.' She thought to herself. She missed him. But that was then, this is now. Time to carry on living. Life is for the living, is what Jeff used to say, and he had lost two whole families before he married Becky. She had lost one husband, but he was a no account, shiftless bum, leaving her with three children and little else. She wouldn't disrespect the dead, but she wouldn't say anything kind about that man either.

She would just keep her mouth shut. Jeff had more than made up for having to live with a tumble weed for five years.

As the wagon bumped and swayed under Jack's steady control of the mules, she thought back to more than a year ago. It started out like any other day, when two strangers rode up to the house. She should have known when they didn't "Hello the house", they were up to no good. She also should have known that they had done something to Jack and little Jeff, as they didn't ride in with them to bring them to the house. It was a rough life out on the plains, and travel was tough. But people took care of one another. Becky had fed many a lone traveler, and even a few families headed out West to the Countries, when Jeff was alive. But Jeff had an uncanny ability to spot ruffians, and hooligans - he would feed them, but watch them with his rifle lazily pointing at them. Once they finished eating, Jeff would take Jack and a second gun, and mosey them along over the hills. There was no Jeff to read the sign in these two men.

She had the girls go in the hidden cellar. Bar the door, and if anyone but me, Jack, or Jeff finds you, don't open it. If they try and open it, shoot right through the door. All three girls were old enough to handle a gun, and all three had Jeff's backbone. They wouldn't be easy prey. She stayed at the door, and greeted the two men. She held the rifle ready, but she knew she would only get one shot, and the way they saddled to each side, so she would have to pick a target, just one, told her all she had to know. One of them, the one on the left started to talk. The other one edging up slowly. She had decided she had run out of time, and was going to take her shot when the one on the right darted at her.

She made a mistake, and turned the gun to take on the one coming at her. She realized her mistake immediately. She wasn't going to get a shot off at either one of them. But she did pull the trigger, and a shot rang out. It hit the dirt and not much else. Then strong mean hands were pulling her off the porch. She tried to punch, scratch, scream, yelling out for Jack and Little Jeff. That just made the two men laugh.

"Your boys are kinda sleeping it off out in the wood line. Briar here, well he hits like a mule. The little one might even be dead." And they laughed again. She screamed out curses, and tried to fight, But these were tough men, in a tough land, muscles and hands hardened from labor and hard times. She was no match, but she wanted to do her Jeff proud, and kept on fighting.

Just as the men started to rip her dress off, one sleeve already dangling helplessly from her wrist, the first of the ten men rounded the corner of the corral. They had heard the shot. They knew there was a cabin and a woman who fed strangers hereabouts, and two of them men had actually eaten a meal with Becky and Jeff, when the girls were much smaller. As the first of the ten men came around the corner, it only took them a second to read the sign. These were Western Men, born and bred in hard times, but none of them would mishandle a woman. They treated family women with great respect, and the girls in the Saloon with almost the same care. Women were precious out in the Wild

Country, and men who forgot that, well, they rarely got a second chance at all.

It was over in less than a minute. Two bad hombres went to meet their maker, and were buried in unmarked graves. Big Bob, the Foreman, wanted to just let the wolves and coyotes take them to their maker. But Old Tom, he was a Christian. He convinced Big Bob that even though these men were evil, the Lord would want them buried and a few words said. Big Bob and the crew agreed, but they drew the line at a marker.

Fast Red, the quickest man with a gun or knife they had ever seen said it best: "God knows where they are, and it is better that no one else does." So they buried them both in the same grave, and left no marker. Old Tom read two lines from his scripture about dust unto dust, but was savvy enough not to mention forgiveness in front of the crew. They found both the boys just inside the wood line. Jack had put up a fight, but the tree limb that knocked him silly lay nearby covered with his blood. Little Jeff, well he was missing a tooth, but was already awake and trying to help his brother when the men found them both.

They were tough boys. Little Jeff helped with the horses, while the men buried the evil doers. Jack, well, he took more than week to heal up correctly, but by then the men were long gone. They stayed two days at the cabin. They fixed the roof, added a room for the girls, and fenced in the corral. Even though they were Cattlemen and Cowboys, not farmers, they cleared an acre for Becky's Truck Garden. Figuring she could trade some vegetables for flour and sugar. Becky had thanked them all.

"No problem, Ma'am." Was all they would say. Like a lot of Western men, they were shy around most respectable women.

Becky heard one of the men say: "You know, I ain't never had a Christmas in my whole life. I heard back East they get presents and a big dinner." The men guffawed and laughed out loud. One of them said: "Yeah, and I heard they got buildings ten feet tall, and trains that go forty miles an hour too!" And they all laughed again. But they quieted up when Becky said:

"It's true. I had a Christmas once in Boston, before we moved out to Ohio. I got an apple, and that Doll right there that my little Cindy takes care of now."

When Becky spoke up, everyone shut up. The doll was passed around. None of the men had seen a real store bought doll from back East. It was the prettiest thing, and Becky had kept it in good shape. Each of her girls got to have the doll for a few years, but they had to take care of it. It was a bit faded, but the lace was still unbroken, the face still had the pretty cheeks and long eyelashes, and the shoes were made out of real leather. All of the men admired it, and got to hold it for a bit. Becky told them all about the grand dinner, the candles on the Tree, and the sugar candies. None of the men had ever had sugar candies, but since they were holding the doll, they had to figure that Becky was not telling a tall tale. It sounded grand to all the men. On the third morning they all left. But Becky never forgot that man's words: "I ain't never had a Christmas in my whole life."

Well, this year he would have one. All of them would. She traded two shirts and pair of pants to get all the fixins for Bear Claws at the Trading Store. If she would make him a batch of Bear Claws too, he would give her two silver dollars. So Becky made up a small batch for the two dollars. She used one dollar to buy the wagon. She gave that man two bear claws too, and well, that put him in such a good mood, he threw in some tack, a buggy whip, and an old cushion. The other dollar she saved for hard times. She had seven dollars in coin money, and a small nugget of gold about the size of her middle knuckle - hidden in the floor. Not even the kids knew it was there.

They came to Dry Gulch, and sure enough, she could see the main campfire from the ridge. It only took about ten minutes before one of the outriders came up to the wagon. It was Fast Red. He recognized her immediately.

"Well How de do, Miss Becky! What are you doing out here in this cold and snow?"

He eyed the wagon with the three pretty girls and the two grown boys in it with undisguised curiosity.

"I brought Christmas for you boys!"

Well, let me tell you, when Big Bob saw all the food, the bear claws (and truth be told, the pretty girls too), it was all he could do to speak. Western men don't cry, but they get damn close on occasion. The boys built the fire up big and proper, and quicker than a jackrabbit could hop they built a big lean to, for the girls, and brought in some logs for stools. Well, when the men were done eating, and the Bear Claws were given out. Two a piece. One to eat now. One for Breakfast, Well, okay Western Men don't cry, but a little puddle of mist did fall from more than one eye among them. They ate in silence. It was the first bear claw (which would come to be called a "donut" in the modern world) they had ever tasted for six of them. Big Bob, Old Tom, Fast Red, and Riley, well they had bear claws in ST. Louis, and swore you could buy them in a shop. They assured Becky tho, that the shop made Bear Claws were not in the same class as hers. That made Becky just beam with pride.

Then she gave out the apples. The men were speechless. A present? Big quiet men had no way to express their feelings, so they just thanked her and put the apples away in saddle bags, hidden in pockets, or under their blankets. But Becky wasn't done just yet.

"Are you all ready for some dancing?"

If God himself had appeared at that moment, the men couldn't have been more surprised. They just stared stupidly at Becky, as if they didn't understand.

Becky spoke up again:

"Jack here is a fair to middling fiddle player. He knows a ton of songs. Ruth, Ethel, Mary and I haven't been to a barn dance since my husband died. We would love to dance. Now if you want to court any of us, well you will just have to come by the cabin proper like. But as for me, I would sure like to dance."

It turned out that Old Tom couldn't dance a lick, but he could sing like an Angel. Riley could play a bit of fiddle so Jack could get in a good stomping or step too. Everyone but Old Tom got several turns dancing with Becky or one of the girls. It seemed the girls got lighter and lighter on their feet as the night wore on. They never got tired, and never refused a dance. Finally, about midnight, the girls gathered in the lean to, the fire grew a little lower, and stories of the trail were told as a reward for the dancing. The girls found out that some of the men had ridden on a train. Two had fought in Indian Wars. Two more had schooling. Real schooling. They could cipher and do numbers.

The girls were fascinated. They had never seen writing before. So Old Tom, he carefully tore an empty page out of his Bible, and with a careful graceful hand, wrote out each of the Girls names and Jack's and Little Jeff's too. He wrote out Becky's name too. He showed them how to trace the letters in the ground, so they could practice. If asked to sign their name, well, within weeks, all the girls, Becky and the two boys could. They could make their mark now, with letters! What a gift.

In the morning, it didn't surprise Becky at all that Fast Red asked permission to court Ruth. She had seen the looks the night before. She was surprised that Old Tom took a shine to Ethel. She got a bigger surprise when Old Tom saddled up to ride home with them. He was done with the Trail. If Ethel would have him, he was meaning to become a farmer. That made Becky smile. The biggest surprise came when Big Bob, the Foreman, asked Becky if he could come a courting. She hadn't seen that coming at all. She had to admit, he was a fine figure of a man. Quiet. Competent. Fair. Like Jeff, but different.

"Becky, I ain't never been married. I have spent more than half my life on the trail. I have saved up a mite. I was going to buy a little spread down in Texas. But, well, if you ain't married off once we get this herd to St. Louis, well, I would like to come back and take your hand in marriage."

Becky surprised herself and set all the men and her children off into fits of hoopin and hollerin, when she brazenly reached up and kissed Big Bob full on the lips.

"Done and Done!" She said.

Which stood as written in stone in the Old West, until the circuit preacher could marry them off proper like.

The man who had said almost two years earlier at Becky's place: "I ain't never had a Christmas in my whole life." Spoke up before they all parted ways:

"I just want to say, Ma'am. If this is what Christmas is like. I want one every year."

Becky didn't hesitate at all.

"Slim, Done and done! You all show up at the Cabin next year, and we will have Christmas. And any other year you can make it."

And they did.

That Night. A story of the Old West

By Kevin Hughes

The Saloon was filled that night. Even respectable town folks, church going, pleasant folk with waxed mustaches and pocket watches, were there that night. Ladies of the Evening stood side by side with real Ladies, and both were treated with respect and courtesy by the men there that night. Everyone who was there, remembered everything that happened that night. So much so that when people referred to what they saw, witnessed, and gaped at while it happened - they simply said: "I was there... That Night."

If you said: "That Night." People knew what you meant. It needed no explanation as to witch night, or what night, or when. In the annals of both Legend and History, it became known simply as: That Night. I know. I was there. That Night.

Hammerin Hank Harper, the King of Bare Knuckle Boxing, had come to Sweetwater two weeks ago. He boasted that he could beat any man, from any where, at any time. And he had. He beat some so bad that they never recovered. Others he beat so bad that they couldn't see right anymore. Some were left crippled. Some were left- dead. Hammerin Hank didn't stop because you went down. He kept on Hammering.

He was a huge man. Fists like Christmas Hams. A jaw built to square. He stood six foot six inches tall, and weighed as much as a pony. For the first time in many people's lives, they saw what the expression "rippling with muscle" meant. Because when Hammering Hank Harper took off his shirt, coiled muscle, like strings of iron rope slid and slithered over ripped cut strips of even more muscle. Hammerin Hank won a lot of fights by merely taking his shirt off.

Women were known to swoon. Some to widen their eyes, flair their nostrils, and lick their lips with an unconscious desire to feel that powerful body. Hammerin Hank Harper took note of those faces. Pity the poor husband who tried to stop him from granting the wife her wish. And pity the poor wife who found to her dismay that he would leave her not in the throws of passion, but thrown up against the wall like an old used blanket, or discarded saddle gear. As bruised and broken as any of the men he had beaten.

People paid to see Hammerin Hank Harper- hoping he would meet his match. The ones who fought him, found they paid too; but in broken bones, blood, and sometimes- their lives. Hammerin Hank wasn't a dirty fighter, merely a mean fighter. A fighter with no remorse. With his power, speed, and strength, he would pummel bigger men like a side of meat, and smaller, quicker men, he would snap like kindling. When you went down under his massive fists, he would then use brick like feet driven by thighs thick enough to be piston rods on the new fangled steam engines- and stomp. He didn't stop hitting, stomping, or moving, until you didn't move anymore.

Blood lust, the musky smell of fear, and being that close to danger not directed at you, was a lure no man- or woman- of the Old West could resist. In a hard land, filled with hard men, strong women, and tough times- someone like Hammerin Hank Harper earned respect, awe, and outright admiration. You took your chances when you tangled with Hammerin Hank, just like you took your chances with weather, the wild, and wolves- or any other force of nature. Until …That Night.

He was a quiet man. Not given to small talk. He did his job and did it well. As big as he was, he never seemed to attract much attention. Like a lot of men in the Old West, he was solid, solitary, steady. Nobody could out work him. Although many tried. He just never seemed to get tired. Nobody could out lift him either. He would pull a calf out of the river and carry it to shore, when the other Ranch Hands would have to use a horse and ropes.

A tip of the hat was all they gave him in acknowledgement- his only reply would be a quick smile. Sometimes, for a really big calf struggling in the mud, he would just duck under it, lift it onto his shoulders, lock his arms around its legs and walk to dry land. The other Cowboys would get off their horses, take off their hats, and bow towards him. He would give them that quick smile, and tap his hat brim with two fingers. Acknowledged.

The quiet man had only one Sister. Becky. He loved her more than any other person. When she married Tyler, well, he was as happy for her as he could be. Tyler was a good man. A man to ride the river with…in winter. Becky and Tyler made a better team than any matched horses the Quiet Man had ever seen.

Every time he was in Sweetwater, he would stay at their place on the outskirts of town. That quick smile of his showing up often at her cooking, Tyler's stories, and both their singing.

He had family. Until...

Tyler came out of the Feed Store. A big man was pawing at Becky perched on the seat of their wagon. He could see on her face she was scared. She wasn't backing down though- she was telling the big man that she was married. She was telling him that he had better leave her alone. That if he wanted those kinds of favors, there was brothel above the Saloon. But the big man wanted her.

Tyler never had a chance. Neither did Becky.

Word got out to the Quiet Man running a small herd twenty miles away. The Foreman let him go- and wished him luck. Thinking he was going to lose the best hand he had ever had. For when the Quiet Man got the news, he asked who did it. The rider simply said: Hammerin Hank Harper. That didn't stop the Quiet man from mounting up. But it got a grunt from the Foreman and the rest of the Cowboys. The Quiet Man was riding to his doom.

Becky was barely able to move when the Quiet Man got to her side. She couldn't talk. Her jaw was busted in four places. A tear leaked from her only good eye. The Quiet Man couldn't even hold her hands. Both of them had been broken in her valiant but futile attempt to stop the inevitable. Her gentle hands were no match for the rock hard head and steel jaw of Hammer Hank Harper.

Tyler was dead from just the one punch. A punch he never expected. Probably never even felt. He might have put up a fight, if he had been ready, or had much experience with bad men. He had neither. A part of his mind couldn't believe how fast that big man turned when Tyler put a strong, but gentle hand on his shoulder and said: "Leave my wife alone."

Those were Tyler's last words. And luckily he never heard the screams and words of his wife , as she struggled under a body to strong, to heavy, and to filled with passion to be denied. But she fought. Hard. So hard that Hammerin Hank Harper had to slap her a couple of times, breaking her jaw and teeth with each ham fisted slap. She broke her own hands as she repeatedly hit is head and face with her hands. Hands meant to nurture, careers, and care. They made lousy weapons.

He had his way with her. And then threw her away. Only when Hammerin Hank Harper went into the Hotel to rest up for his first challenge of the evening, did the good people of Sweetwater venture out to the wagon. They lifted Tyler's body onto the backboard. Then put Becky's still breathing body next it. Reverend Kelly, and his wife took the wagon and its sad contents back out to the ranch. Little Red, Sparky, and Old Tom, the three Ranch Hands at Tyler's little spread took over. Little Red is the one that lit out on a horse to find the Quiet Man.

For three days the Quiet Man sat at his sister's side. He let Nelly, the Reverend's wife, tend to the womanly needs of his sister's battered, bruised, beaten body. He took care of everything else. He cooked. He kept the ranch running. He buried Tyler -

propper like. He combed his sister's hair, like he did when they were kids. And he talked to her. A lot.

He kept trying to get some life back into her eyes. He brought up every good memory he could. He told her stories about their Mom - a woman that didn't live long enough to know Becky, or Becky her. Those stories used to make Becky smile and laugh. He told her she had to live. That Tyler would want her to stay strong. He told her he needed her.

He talked more in those three days than he had talked in his entire life. And then some. He hoped she could hear him. But the light never came back in her eyes. Or eye. For only the one eye worked, and it was alway full of a tear. Until that night. Her eye went flat. Lifeless. A moment later so did her body.

The Quiet Man built her box, while the ranch hands dug a whole next to Tyler's grave. The Reverend and his wife, the three Cowboys, and the Quiet Man filled in the dirt without a sound. The Reverend put his hand on the Quiet Man's shoulder.

"What are you going to do now?"

The Quiet Man said nothing. He just looked at the Reverend, who stepped back at the flatness in the Quiet Man's Eyes. As the Quiet Man rode off to town, the Reverend told his wife and the three Cowboys to mount up.

'I just saw the Devil. We have to follow."

Hammerin Hank Harper was warming up. He had already beaten two would be "winners" in less than twenty seconds. He didn't even have to take his shirt off, or dirty his boots. Those two dirt suckers had been pulled out before he could stomp them. That was okay with Hammerin Hank Harper- for they didn't even land a punch, so why would they deserve a stomping?

He did have a light sweat covering his body with a silvery sheen; making him look like some God had stepped out of the river: dripping, deadly, magnificent. Women looked at that body with open invitation, men looked with envy, and more than a little fear. It made Hammerin Hank Harper preen.

The door to the Saloon opened. The Quiet Man stood there. Eyes flatter than the darkest night up on the Mesa. A coldness filled the room. Everyone there felt it. Even Hammerin Hank Harper. Whatever that man in the doorway brought with him, it was heavy. It was dark. It was destiny. And it weighed in the air like the wet air before a tornado. Brooding. Expanding. Poised.

No one breathed. No one moved. Except Hammerin Hank Harper - who turned to look at the Quiet Man. Not an ounce of fear in either. Hammerin Hank Harper merely raised one eyebrow in a curious gesture. The Quiet Man said one word:

"Becky."

Hammerin Hank Harper uttered in genuine surprise what was to be his last words:

"Becky who?"

41

The Quiet Man didn't move. Everyone there that night swore to it on a stack of bibles. One minute he was standing in the door of the Saloon. The next moment he was standing in front of Hammerin Hank Harper. The Quiet Man's open hand slapped Hammerin Hank Harper on the side of his face. That first slap did three things in a row:

It dislocated the square iron jaw of Hammerin Hank Harper.

It sent teeth and blood, and Hank- flying a good six feet down the bar with out Hank's boot touching the floor once.

It brought fear, for the first time in Hammerin Hank's Life, to the surface.

Hank had barely regained his balance, as his body coiled with anger to strike back, when the second slap landed. This time on the other side of Hank's face. And just like the first slap, it did three things:

It unhinged the square iron jaw of Hammerin Hank Harper.

It sent teeth, blood, and Hank- flying a good six feet down the bar- in the opposite direction, without Hank's boots touching the floor once.

Hank had barely enough time to turn back towards the Quiet Man when the third slap landed. Then the fourth. And a fifth. By then Hank's mind had shifted from fear to terror. This creature that was attacking him, seemed hell bent on slapping him to death.

A few minutes later, and Hammerin Hank Harper (who still hadn't landed a punch, because he hadn't shown any) realized that he was being slapped like one of the girls he liked to take from their puny husbands. Just like those women, he just wanted it to end. But it didn't.

Hank felt the cold water, the burning of liquor going down his throat. He sputtered, threw his arms out to get his balance, only to be surpassed by the fact that he wasn't standing. He was laying on the floor in a puddle of his own blood, a smattering of teeth, and even a few shards of bone. It was hard for him to see, since everything seemed to be bleary - and there were two of everything.

He watched in slow motion as the Quiet Man came into focus. Hammerin Hank Harper could only watch in awe as the Quiet Man lifted him in one smooth arc from the floor to his full height. The Quiet man didn't stop there. His arm continued to lift Hammering Hank clear of the ground, then up almost eight feet into the air.

It was the most impressive display of strength that Hammerin Hank Harper had ever seen. For the Quiet Man had lifted him with no more effort than Hammerin Hank would have used to lift a horseshoe. It was only then that Hammerin Hank Harper saw the fist coming up from belt high towards his ribs. A moment ago he thought he had seen the most impressive display of strength he had ever seen, well…now he felt it.

The punch landed like a cannonball. Exploding half of Hammerin Hank's ribcage like a busted melon. He could feel his innards burst, a rush of blood, snot and air flew out of his nose and mouth. Pointy ends of broken ribs sawed through the side of those coiled muscles Hank used to be so proud of. The pain was incredible. It hurt as bad as the realization that Hammerin Hank Harper was helpless to stop the next blow, or the next. He felt things move and shift under his skin, bones pounded to powder, organs popping like so many pig bladders, air leaking not from his mouth and nose, but wheezing out gaping wounds in the sides of his chest, and the small of his back.

And still the blows came. And came. And came.

Then the first of his arm bones broke,then another. Another. Still the Quiet Man wouldn't let him fall. Holding Hank upright with one arm of Iron, the other fist of Iron was wreaking its fury on any remaining unbroken stubborn bones. Hammerin Hank Harper had ceased making any Human sounding cries minutes ago, or maybe it was hours. Hank had no conception of Time anymore. Just pain, agony and a constant prayer to make it all stop.

Hank didn't think he could feel any more pain, or scream any louder. He was wrong. Because just then the Quiet Man broke the first of his leg bones. Hank had heard that the most painful injury a man could have , was a broken femur. Now he knew that was true- twice. No longer capable of making any human sounds or thoughts, Hammerin Hank Harper was reduced to animal sounds: grunts, shrieks, howls… and still the Quiet man vented controlled fury on the rubbery water filled sack in front of him. A sack that used to be Human, or similar to one.

No one who was there That Night, would ever forget. How could they? When the Quiet Man stopped- finally. The only part of Hammerin Hank Harper that resembled any part of a Human Being, was his boots. When the Doctor was called, to make an official ruling. He simply stared at the goo on the floor and asked:

"What is that?"

The Quiet Man rode back to the Ranch. He knelt next to his Sister's grave. A week later he toppled over. They buried him next to his Sister and Tyler.

Stories are still told about That Night.

Around campfires all over the West, bad men take pause, knowing the Quiet Man might come back. Good men wish he would.

The Shooter- Ghost Story of the Old West

By Kevin Hughes

He did not feel the first bullet. It went through the fleshy part of his stomach. The second bullet didn't make much of an impact on him either. That bullet went through the meaty part of his thigh without hitting anything major. The third bullet sliced through the muscle between his neck and shoulder. None of them slowed the Shooter down, or threw off his aim.

Even with three bullet wounds, and dozens of rounds whistling by, the Shooter kept his feet braced, his guns level, and his sights clear. Each click of the chamber from his Colt 45 signaled another man would die. Click. Death. Click. Death. Click. Death. Click. Death. Click. Death. Click. Death. Six clicks, six dead men. And still the bullets came for him.

Click. Nothing. The absence of noise was the loudest sound in the room. The Shooters gun was empty. Not all the targets were down. Not by a long shot, or many shots. The Shooter knew when it started it had to end this way. There were too many of them and only six shots in his pistol. He would have to reload. He knew when he tried to reload, at that range, with that many people shooting at him...well, it just wasn't his deal.

After that empty click, the bar froze for half a second. Long enough for the smoke to lift. What it revealed was six dead men laying in puddles of their own blood on a sawdust covered floor.

One spittoon had spilled over close to a dead body, making it look like the man had just spit his last chaw. Another man was slumped over a card table, looking more like a drunk who had one drink too many, than a man who had one bullet too many. A third man leaned up against the bar, as dead as the brass railing that was holding him up, with his gun still dangling from lifeless fingers.

More than a dozen men were still standing. The rest of the Bad Bill Meyers Gang. Bill, Thadeus, and Cleo, the baddest of the Bad Bill Meyers gang were dead. They died in that first round of gunfire. As did: Red, Harp, and Jeremiah. Like the coyotes they were, the dozen or so men left standing, smelled blood. The Shooter was leaking from three wounds, he was still standing-loading his six shooter with quick sure hands. But they knew he would never pull that trigger again.

Later, everyone admitted they had never seen anyone reload in the middle of a fire fight as quickly and calmly as the Shooter did that night. He was loading his sixth round before the surprise at the empty click ended. And with it, a fusillade of bullets rained into his body like hail on the open plain.

The first bullet to do serious damage hit his right hip, just below his gun belt - twisting his body to one side. A dozen bullets rammed into his chest and shoulder and back on his exposed right side, spinning him in a complete circle. He was already dead, but trying to pull his gun up to level - to shoot at least one more of the men peppering his body with lead. He didn't make it. Later the

Doctor said the Shooter had more than forty bullets in him when he died.

But he spoke one last sentence with his last breath. A sentence that chilled everyone in the bar. A sentence that stalks the old West until this day. A sentence that was both a dying man's last words, and a promise:

"I'll be back."

****

Josh, Regan, and Cap, gathered up the rest of the remaining Bad Bill Meyers Gang in the hills outside of Sweetwater. It had been six months since the Shooter took their three older brothers, and three of the baddest of the Bad Bill Meyers Gang down. Each with a single shot from his six shooter. If the Shooter had only carried two guns, instead of just one, well, they might not be here now. But that was the past. Tonight was the first night of the future.

The Gang was back in Business. Josh, Regan and Cap, kept the name of their band of outlaws out of respect for their older brother Bill. But Bill, Thaddeus and Cleo were soft hearted compared to the younger brothers. The original Bad Bill Meyers gang never went after women, or children, or ranchers. They just robbed stagecoaches, trains, and banks. The younger brothers had no such limitations. They were cruel mean tough hombres.

Evil can cut men deep and wide too. And these were Western Men, as raw, hard, and tough as the land around them. They had no give. No mercy. No souls. Many a woman died at their pleasure, not hers. Many a child looked up wide eyed to see the barrel of a gun or rifle pointed at them. A moment later they looked only up at the sky with a smoking hole where their thoughts used to be. The original Bad Bill Meyer Gang got a new name. One not of their choosing, but it stuck. They were called what they were: The Younger Brothers.

When Josh first heard a man scream: "It is the Younger Brothers! Run!" In that little town of Dry Gultch Arizona, it made him smile. He shot that man in the leg, just so he could ask him why he screamed: "It is the Younger Brothers." The man lay whimpering looking up at the big man on the horse standing over him. He knew he wasn't going to live much longer. So he told the truth.

"Everyone calls your gang the Younger Brothers. Some folks don't even think you are Human. They think Satan sent his minions out West to do his dirty work. People think you are demons."

Well, that made Josh and his two brothers laugh out loud. Just before they shot the wounded man Josh leaned over his horse, looked down at the man, pointed his pistol at his head and said out loud (over the sounds of his brother's laughter):

"You tell the Devil, when you see him momentarily (and all the gang laughed at that), that if'n he wants to ride with the Younger Brothers, he is welcome. As long as he brings whiskey and women folks."

A shot rang out, and the message was delivered first hand.

****

She knew it was a risk. Everyone had told her. The Frontier wasn't the place yet for pretty girls with schooling and upbringing. But she was stubborn, and her husband was young and Foolish. She thought teaming up with the three other wagons would make them all safe. But the other men knew how tough it could get out on the trail. They tried to tell her, her husband, and her two little sisters that the trail was no place for tenderfeet like them. And besides, said the Trail Boss:

"The Younger Brothers just shot up a town not forty miles from where we get water and supplies. If they catch us, with all you pretty girls bunched up…Well, there ain't no telling what they will do to all of you until they tire of it."

"You won't let that happen though, will you?"

Said the pretty woman with the schooling but no education.

"Ma'am, we won't be able to stop it."

She was aghast.

"Why not?"

"Because by then, Ma'am, we will all be dead."

He tipped his hat and walked off to the lead wagon.

The Trail Boss had been right. They were all dead. Brave men. They fought hard. It didn't help. There were only seven men with the wagons, including her husband. Her husband had never fired a gun in his life. And he never got a chance to. He got shot trying to get into the wagon to get his rifle. The Trail Boss told him he should always carry his rifle, that it needed to be handy if trouble started. He didn't listen to the Old Trail Boss - but he did learn a powerful lesson - you should always keep your rifle with you out on the Frontier. He paid for that lesson with his life.

She was trying to be brave so her two little sisters would be brave too. Becky May (who was only seventeen), and sweet little Mary (fourteen), huddled with her, hugging her tight. All the men were dead. Some of the Younger Brother's gang had taken Mrs. Parsons, and Old Mother Thatcher out beyond the firelight. The screams were terrible at first, especially when accompanied by raucous laughter from the men causing those screams. It seemed to go on for hours.

Finally, the screaming stopped. Six of the men came back to the fire, laughing and hitching up their gun belts. She pulled her little sisters closer. None of them looked at the men, but they couldn't close their ears to stop hearing what the men said. What they bragged about doing to those poor women, how the women had pleaded for mercy - and then begged later that they would do anything the men wanted if they just wouldn't hurt them anymore.

And finally, the women just begged to die. And they did.

She and her little sister had heard every word. And they heard what those same men said to them when they came back:

"You three are the cream of the crop. Why when Josh, Reagan and Cap get here, they are going to give us all a bonus for saving you for them."

Another voice chirped in, in a chilling glimpse of the future:

"And if you are still breathing, or able to move a bit, they might let us have you for the rest of the night!"

That set the men to laughing out loud, as another voice said:

"As pretty as those three are, I ain't particular that they still be alive."

Fear and bile rose in equal amounts in the throats of the three young women. They didn't cry out. They were being brave for each other. But their fears were real, and their worst fears were riding into camp. They heard the horses before they saw the men. When the men dismounted and walked to the fire the three girls stood up and faced them.

"Well, well, well. Looky here boys. The Candy store has come to us!"

Josh turned to his gang.

"You boys did good. (His face darkened for a bit) None of you took some of this candy before we got here now, did you?"

Twenty two men nodded as one:

"No Josh, Cap, Reagan. No sir. We took our pleasure from the Old Lady and the Teacher's wife. They didn't put up much of a fight afore they died."

Josh nodded. Then he looked over at the three young women, one of them just barely a woman now. Cap and Reagan looked over too.

"Well, I think we can trust these little ones to fight a bit longer. And maybe we will keep them alive for a few days, so everyone can have some candy."

And all the men laughed, hooted, and hollered. Until…

****

They heard his voice first. Twenty or more guns snapped from holsters as the men holding them looked out into the night. The voice sounded familiar to some of the men, but not all. And the voice was calm, sure, and getting closer.

"Well Boys, I don't think anyone is getting any candy tonight. But you will get what you deserve."

"What the hell are you talking about? You can have some too, or you can die. Those are your choices."

The voice grew closer, got stronger, and more confident.

It even laughed a soft light laugh.

"Oh, I don't think so. I make my choices. You made yours."

And with that he stepped out into the firelight.

"Oh sweet mother of God. It's the Shooter! "

Tex didn't mean to say that out loud, but he did.

Josh wasn't scared, just curious.

"Tex, what do you mean? He is the Shooter?"

"Josh, I swear on my Mother's Grave and the Good God's Bible, that is the man we killed in Sweetwater. The Shooter. He killed Bill, Thaddeus and Cleo that night, and the other three, while you Younger brothers were over in Tombstone. "

Josh, Reagan and Cap turned as one:

"That true? You the one what killed our brothers?"

The Shooter smiled.

"Yes. And now I am going to kill you. All of you."

He didn't say it as a boast. He wasn't bragging. He was stating a fact.

A moment went by, and the Shooter spoke again:

"Those of you who didn't take any Candy can leave. The rest of you will stay here forever."

Two of the men closest to the Horses jumped up on the backs of the nearest horses and high tailed it out of there. A minute later and three more men did the same. Josh didn't even turn to watch them ride away.

Cap said:

"Josh, you gonna let them light out like that?"

"No. Cap. Don't worry. We can catch them later, after we take care of this man. When we do, well, they won't ever ride away again. It is still twenty of us, and one of him. And we have our guns out."

"So do I."

Everyone blinked. Even the three girls still huddled together as close as fear and their bodies would let them, blinked.

When did he draw? Nobody saw it. One second he was talking to the Younger Brother's, the next he was holding his colt 45, level, unshaken, and aimed right a the heart of Josh.

Josh was evil, cruel, mean to the skinny, but he wasn't stupid. He knew the man had to be fast, he never saw a draw like that. But he also knew that his two brothers and him were dead shots. None of them ever missed. That was true of at least six other members of the Younger Brothers. There was no way, at this range, and with this many guns aimed at him, that the Shooter would get off more than a single shot.

Josh's finger tightened on his trigger, the smile on his face was all the signal his brother's needed. The night erupted with the flame of gunfire. Twenty two men died that night. Each and every one, shot once. Through the heart. One man road away. Three women knelt in prayer.

****

It was six years later. The house and barn had stood for almost five of those years. She was married now. So was her middle sister. The youngest sister was being courted by a nice young man who had the ranch just a few miles outside of town. It was hot that day. Much hotter than usual.

Her man was out by the well. Cutting up a chord of wood with powerful blows from his Ax. He would split each log with one swift cut, bend over and throw the two pieces into the growing pile on the wagon. Then pick up another log, and do the same. She loved watching his body as it gleaned with sweat while the muscles under his skin rippled like oil on water. She loved that man.

He was the quietist, most gentle, most loving man, she had ever known, met, or heard of. Nobody but her ever saw him without his shirt on. He made sure of that. He wasn't shy. She knew that. She also knew why he didn't want anyone to see his bare skin.

There were three bullet holes in his neck, side, and thigh. And fifty puckered entrance and exit wounds on his back and chest. He should be dead. He wasn't. She smiled at the memory of him riding up to them all that first sunrise - three girls, scared, lonely, still in shock, sitting next to a dead fire; surrounded by twenty two dead bodies. He had walked right up to her, took her hand, kissed it lightly and said:

"It is time to take you home. There won't be anymore trouble."

And there wasn't.

He is the Shooter.

The Shootout

By Teresa Carlson

Carson Boone was a 19 year old modern day cowboy who rarely shoots a gun. Now he is facing off with the Sheriff in a shootout for some Native American gems. "Go get him baby." The sheriff's wife said as she handed him his pistol and walked to the sidelines to watch. "You ready son?" The Sheriff asked as Carson nervously twisted his gun around. "Last chance to back down and take your arse home in one piece." The sheriff said as he rolled the bullets in the revolver holder and turned to his wife to say something to her.

Carson swallowed the lump in his throat as he rolled the barrel to see how many bullets he had to use. He could feel the pit in his stomach as he saw that there were no bullets In his gun. He quickly put two and two together and realized the sheriff was cheating him. The sheriff needed him out of the way to have the Native American gems. A shootout would make it seem like the sheriff won fair and square with no questions asked. Carson quickly looked at the sheriff to make sure he wasn't looking before he looked for his best friend Artie Ace in the crowd. "I have no gun." Carson mouthed to Artie as a last attempt to get help before the shootout. Carson watched as Artie nodded his head and nonchalantly disappeared into the crowd.

"Let's do this. 10 step walk and then turn around and shoot." The sheriff explained as we put our backs against each other and began the dead man's walk. "One, two, three, four, five, six, seven, eight, nine…….." The Sheriff went quiet. No gun shots, just silence. Carson slowly turned and saw the Sheriff staring at him with a smirk. "I got him Carson!" Artie yelled as he shot the Sheriff straight in the heart. "Nooooo!" We heard the Sheriff's wife yell as she sobbed and ran to her husband's aid. "You did this!" The wife screamed as Carson pushed her aside and grabbed the Native American jewels from the dead Sheriff's pocket. "No one messes with the sheriff's family." His wife said as she grabbed my hand. Carson pushed her off and ran back to Artie and the horse Artie managed to get. Carson and Artie rode off with a heavy but fulfilled heart as they discussed how to keep the gems safe from now on.

The Blade

By Kevin Hughes

It was just there. One second it wasn't. The next…it was. Six inches of tempered steel buried to the hilt.

Unfortunately, six inches of tempered steel, buried to the hilt in a human chest, is almost invariably fatal.

It was this time too.

Everybody had seen Bad Bart go for his gun. Nobody saw the Blade throw his knife.

Bart only had a moment to look down, before his empty hands had reached to pull the knife out of his chest.

They never made it. His life force only started the movement, his death ended it.

He did not crumble. Nor did he slide to the ground.

He just sort of folded in on himself, twisted to one side, and died. Just like that. One second he was alive, proud, angry.

The next second…he was not.

There was complete silence in the bar. It was an unusual sound for a Saloon. It might have been because the twenty or so living people in the room were all holding their breath. And the other one, wasn't breathing at all. The only normal sound of breathing came from the Blade, as he looked around the room. Everyone looked away as his eyes registered their presence, deemed them harmless, and moved on. In that room were seven men who had killed before, not one of them was a threat to the Blade. Even the former Captain, a survivor of the Battle of Bull Run, a man as far from cowardice as the moon is from the sun, made sure that the stranger knew he was no threat either.

The lone woman in the room was the first to take in a breath. When she let it out, it was to say: "Thank you, Quiet."

Quiet merely nodded. He knew she meant it. He wasn't given to words much. He didn't often have something to say, so he didn't. It is how he got his nickname: "Quiet." Folks back East thought the nickname was do to his prowess with a knife, a silent weapon. It wasn't. Sure, the screams of the men who died at the end of his blade were silent cries, for it is hard to scream with either your throat slit, or six inches of tempered steel stuck in your heart. The people out West called the Stranger - "Blade" when his knife was out, "Quiet, " when it wasn't.

In towns all across the Old West, there were legends and saying a plenty:

"If Quiet comes into town, don't let the Blade come out." "Quiet ain't never looked for no fight, but Blade has finished them all." "You won't see the Blade until the handle is sticking out."

"Why, I seen Blade throw three knives, one each at the Harrow gang. Each knife thrown so daggum hard ,it took two men to pull the blades out. He pinned the one Harrow boy right to the pillar he was standing in front of. Me and another fella held that Barrow boy's arms up, so two other guys could pull the knife out of the wood. All the while Blade just stood there, waiting for us to bring him back his knives."

Nobody listening, and they all listened to the Old Timer, because they knew the story was true. Most of them were there the night he killed Bad Bart. They all knew that only Quiet could pull a blade free of a body with one hand. For Quiet had showed them a "trick" once, so as he wouldn't have to kill a man who had to little sense, and to much liquor in him. It was six or seven months ago...

Quiet had ridden into town to get some grub. He got his supplies and went to the Saloon to get some home cooking. That Saloon was famous in that part of the country, because old Mrs. Harper cooked not only meals, but pies, and even made bear claws once a month. A meal could cost as much as Fifty Cents. Nobody minded the price. Nobody messed with Mrs. Harper either (Yes, she was the woman who thanked Quiet, when Blade went away), she was both a treasure- and treasured. If the way to a man's heart was through his stomach, she had all their hearts. But...I am wandering off the story of the "trick."

When the drunk had made enough remarks to rouse even Quiet to speak, everyone expected Blade to come out, and a blade too. Instead Quiet just pulled the drunk down into a chair by the big wooden poker table. Quiet slapped the drunk once, which sobered him up right quick.

"Now you watch this close. "

The words were meant for the drunken man, but everyone is the room drew closer to both see, and hear. That was about the most words any of them had ever heard Quiet say, and Blade didn't speak, he acted. But Quiet wasn't done talking:

"You see these two knives?"

People moved back a bit, the blades were out, but Blade didn't appear to be. But…just to be safe…they all became statue like.

"Now, I am going to put them both through the table. One quick like, and one slow like. "

TWINNNGGGGG.

It happened so fast, nobody saw how he did it. One second the knife was on the table, the next second, it was right through it. Just singing like a tuning fork, as it hummed like it was happy to go through four inches of solid oak, in one swift, powerful, stroke.

"That was the quick like. Now this is the slow like."

This time, they all watched as Quiet picked up the second blade, placed the tip of the tempered steel against the four inches of solid oak. He didn't wiggle the knife, like some might have, he didn't use small chopping motions, as some might have. He simply...well... PRESSED the blade deeper into the wood. After the first inch or so seemed to melt into the wood, a small flame burst up to rush around Quiet's flesh. Quiet ignored the flame and kept pressing. The knife just sunk, there is no other word for it, the knife just sunk until the only part above the table top was the hilt. And it was hot.

Quiet spoke again:

"Now, these are good blades. See the groove? That is for the blood to find a way out, when they go inside your body. Other wise, well, I could only put them two inches or so into your body. But since they both have channels to let the pressure of your innards out, well, they slide in just so buttery. So here's the trick. I don't think your body is as strong as this table, nor as thick. Yet I put my blades thru it both quick like and slow like. If you say another word tonight, or have another drink well, here's the trick. I will have to choose to put one thru you slow like, or quick like- and I hate making decisions on an empty stomach. "

The drunken man? Well, he didn't say a word, he just up and left. Quiet went back to his table to eat. He left the blades in the table.

"Quiet, you left your blades in the table!" Yelled out the Old Timer.

Quiet smiled.

"I know Old Timer. I figure if anyone one man can pull out either blade, I shall by them dinner from Mrs. Harper."

They all tried. Even Big John, the Swede, who was the biggest man any of them had ever seen, and the town's Blacksmith. A man so strong he could put his anvil in a wagon without any help at all. And that anvil weighed 400 lbs if it weighed a feather. The Swede tried so hard, he started speaking in Swedish. Martin, the Stone Mason, with a grip like Iron tongs, well he couldn't budge them either. Mrs. Harper wasn't going to have to cook for any of them.

Quiet let them have their fun. Then he walked over to the table, and pulled one knife out with his left hand, and one with right. No trouble at all. Smooth, like sliding a smooth stone down an ice covered stream. Forty pairs of eyes tried to leave their heads, and just as many balls shriveled up. The eyes saw what they saw, turned it into raw fear, the men's testicles did the rest. How strong was Quiet?

Quiet put the blades away. Looked around the room...smiled as he put on his hat, and left them with these few words:

"If you stick them in, you got to learn to take them out."

The end

The Stranger and the Saloon Door

By Kevin Hughes

The doors burst open, flung aside by the power and fury of a human body being propelled thru the air by a far stronger, more powerful, and much more angry human body.

It was a common occurrence in many of the Old Saloons of the Old West- to have a body flung like something insignificant thru the doors, probably over something insignificant. Most saloon doors of the Old West were hinged to swing freely in any direction. Just because a human body left the saloon broken, bloody, damaged, sometimes beyond repair- is no reason to make the doors suffer too. If Saloon Doors could only talk...or can they?

It was dark, as it often was at night out West. After all, there was no electricity in the Old West, nor streetlights, nor gas lamps, well maybe in Kansas City, or out in California, say in High Fallutin San Francisco... maybe. But out here, in towns like : Dry Gulch, Sweetwater, Tombstone, Durango, Siler Station, Laramie, Casper, and a thousand other towns across the Nations, or the Territories...well, the only light at night was in a saloon- outside the shadow ruled, running along side the night like cousins with a wheel and a stick. When the doors of that saloon opened, and closed quickly, no head would turn, there wasn't any trouble in a quick swinging door.

No, sirree. It was when just one door opened, and stayed open, that the folks in the Saloon would stop, turn and look. For when a door froze like that, often a stranger stood silhouetted by the lamps in the door way. One hand holding the door wide, the other, free to reach for his gun. When a door did not swing, but only opened, it was a sure sign that a stranger had stopped to survey the room. Just like the room stopped to survey the man in the doorway. For any time a door was held open, it was likely held open by a Stranger.

Strangers, in the Old West, were always suspect even if they weren't one. Strangers often meant trouble, even if they were not looking for it. Like this Stranger. He wasn't looking for trouble, just a drink, a bite to eat and a bunk for the night. But…if trouble wanted to come hunting, he would be easy to find.

The men of the Old West were hard weathered men. Men who's hands were toughened by hard work done on long days. They were men who carried guns knowing how to use them, and when. They were tough, rangy, mean, a creature just at home on the range as: a wolf, or a mountain lion, or a bear, or a rattlesnake. And…just as deadly. These are men who had looked death in the eye with a steady stare, and a calm heart. "What will be, will be, but I ain't going down without a fight." They never actually said that out loud, but they may as well have. Even the Devil might think twice before taking on some of the hombres that called both the Old West and the Saloons- Home.

That is why, when that door squeaked open, then stopped, as if trying desperately not to come to the attention of the huge calloused hand, holding it lightly open it was surprising to see so many men of the Old West...wither. Their brave independence, and willingness to fight... withering like a dried tumbleweed in the desert under the steady gaze of eyes that only shone with the stark coldness of a desert night.

Those eyes were deserted to, orbs emptied of any fear, of any consequence, of any outcome. It made men at the bar open a slot...a wide slot. It made the men with families decide to call it an early evening. It made tough guys tighten their gun belts, and hope that they wouldn't have to prove tonight that the fast die young. Trouble might run ahead of the Stranger, but never at him. Not directly. Not if trouble wanted to live.

He was a big man. Shoulders cut from canyons, and honed by hard times, his face all edges and planes, like the mountains he felt home in. His muscles didn't run in slabs, but in iron ripped cords of wire. Arms and shoulders that could, without much effort, tear the door off its hinges, fling it a good twenty feet out into the street, fists like baked hams, but harder than cement, hands that could tear down the meatlocker of any man brave, or more likely...foolhardy enough to challenge them.

Bareknuckled he had crushed the bones of many skulls, jaws, sending teeth out the door moments before the bloody battered face of their former owner followed. No, this was not a man you wanted to face, with a gun, or with your fists. The door, even though it was inanimate...quivered.

When the big man. The silent man. The deadly man. The Stranger, glided to the bar with the ease and balance of an athlete, and the poise of a killing machine with the safety off- no one said a word. Except the door. The door breathed quietly, knowing it was safe. For that Stranger would walk out calmly, even if a body or two came out in a hurry, with a broken jaw, or riddled with bullets , before him. The door, at least, would live another day.

It was an innocent remark. Or could have been. Or might have been. We will never know. We do know it was said. Once it was out, it lost all innocence. Like the wife of a farmer, when her husband was asleep, and strong young hands brought pleasure while he slept on through the night. What happens in the night, stays in the night. And so, it started:

" I will have clear water, if you have any."

"Water? " Snorted one of the men who had checked his gun belt: " Real men don't drink much water around here."

Everyone laughed. Even the Stranger.

"Well, I can't rightly say I am a real man. I can say I am a thirsty man. I rode for three days across that desert, without any water. "

Had it stopped there, well, it would have been a quiet night of drinking, card playing, and people minding their own business. It did not stop there. For some men are afraid to show they are afraid. The man who had made the water remark, was one of those men.

"Well, if you are stupid enough to try that desert without water, you sure enough will want water. There ain't no way, in that desert heat, that you rode three days without water. Not and walk in here under your own power. "

There are a lot of things you can call a man out in the Old West. Liar...is...not...one … of …them. The room grew deadly quiet, and that, my friends, is the correct adverb- deadly. Everyone knew it. The bartender placed water in front of the Stranger.

"It's clean water. Sweet water. I have a well out back that is fed from a mountain spring. Since you been in the desert for three days, best you sip it slow. No charge if you tell us all the story about how you came to be without water. I don't mark you as a tenderfoot. Only a tenderfoot would get caught out there without water. So, I imagine there is a story there, one worth the telling."

The Stranger smiled. He knew the old bartender was smart and had been ridden hard and put away wet a few times. He tipped his hat to the old man in respect. It would have been enough of a distraction to let the young tough go on living. Men of the Old West love a story, and would have listened to the Stranger with delight. The Stranger was even willing to tell the story, because the three men beat him and took his water, well, they weren't able to tell the story. After all, it is hard for dead men to talk.

"Much obliged. " He sipped the water slowly. " Let me wet my throat a bit...and I will tell you how I came to be without a canteen, no horse, and sore. When I finally got my horse back, there weren't no water in the canteen. "

The young tough, made another remark, his last, as it turned out.

"Oh, this ought to be good. Let me guess, somebody got the drop on you, beat you, stole your horse, and left you to die. But you being tough and all, followed them on foot, tracked them, and took back your horse. I suppose they just let you mosey on up to their campfire, take your horse and gun, but wouldn't give you a canteen, and told you if you could hold out, there is a town three days away -if'n you can make it there. " He leaned back his head and howled. A few other joined in.

The Stranger's voice changed. It became metal on an anvil. His eyes went as dead black as the night, his body just as quiet. Danger quiet, like when wildlife stops drawing attention to itself in the wild. Birds stop chirping. Squirrels freeze, and bugs hide. That kind of quiet. To still to be natural.

" That's about right. Except they forgot to take my gun. A stray bullet from one of them, mine all hit what I was aiming for, went through all four canteens they had set aside by the coffee. That coffee was the last drink I had. (There was a pause, as the Stranger took a long, slow, soft swallow of the sweet water.) Come to think of it, it was the last drink those three fellas had too. " The smile that came on the Stranger's Face would have made the Devil cringe. It was empty of remorse, bereft of passion, not an ounce of forgiveness in it.

The men who could see the Stranger's face, never forgot that smile. It followed them into their dreams almost every night.

The tough knew he had gone to far, but he wasn't stopping now. He had no backdown in his backbone- just like he had no sense in his head. It is a bad combination if you want to live to see another day. He made his third, and final remark of the evening:

"So you braced there men with your guns there (pointing to the twin holsters slung low on the narrow waist of the big man) and shot them before they got their guns out?"

The Stranger sill wearing that same smile, except now, there was no one at the bar, but the stranger and the young tough.

"No. I kept my guns in my holster, just like I am doing now. I let them take their guns out. Just like I am going to let you. Only then, will I pull out my guns. "

The young tough couldn't believe it. He knew that he was fast, at least three of the "fastest guns in the West" found out they weren't when they challenged him. And this Stranger was going to let him draw first? The smile on his face was one of a man counting his chickens before they hatched. He laughed. And pulled his gun out. He saw it come out, saw it become level, and still the Stranger had not moved. He thought for a moment, that was very strange. Did the Strange want to die? Then he tightened his finger on the trigger. He never saw the Strangers guns come out. He did feel the bullets hitting him one, after another, after another. Backing him up to the Saloon doors.

He tried to reach up, guns forgotten, to hold onto the doors, for a brief moment he did hold himself erect using the saloon doors, much like Christ must have used the Cross, for support as the life drained out of him. "Sweet Jesus…." were his last words. Then another volley of bullets drove him out in to the darkness of a Western Town at night. It was still again, both inside the saloon, and outside. The night shadows made the body in the street into the nothingness that it now was.

Inside, the big stranger had both his guns out, still smoking. Nobody but him, and the dead tough… knew that ten bullets had been fired. In the morning, men who could face a bear with nothing but a knife and a frying pan, would turn green and vomit. Ten bullets. Ten. Six in the heart, not the chest, the heart. Four…four, in what used to be the space between the dead man's eyes. No one had ever seen shooting like that. Nobody ever wanted to.

The big man let his guns cool, as he looked around the room. The bartender put another glass of sweet water up on the bar.

"I suppose we won't be needing that story after all. You can bunk out back, there is a bunk room in the barn. You can bar the door from the inside."

"Much obliged old man. I thank you for that. I don't think I need to bar the door"…and he looked around the room.

The old man bartender laughed out loud:

'No, no. I suppose not. "

The saloon door stayed quiet.

Dusty: A tale of the old West

By Kevin Hughes

His name was not always Dusty. Back East, they called him: William Henry Buckley, which is quite the handle.

He wasn't very tall. With boots on, he could boast to be five foot six inches tall. He had rust red hair, like old barbed wire, or a worn down barn. Freckles, lay like spots of dust, all across his face, neck, and shoulders, but just a sprinkle, a light dusting- if you will. He was much stronger than he looked. Which many a bigger man found out, just a bit to late. He wasn't wiry, or willow thin, but he wasn't solid oak, or heavily muscled either. He was a medium build, but on the lighter side. He had wide shoulders for his size, and a narrow waist that all Western Men seem to have no matter where they were born. He was quiet, a good listener too. It wasn't that he didn't like to talk, it is just that most of his life there wasn't anybody to talk too. Back East Dusty was a minor clerk, in a minor counting house, out West, Dusty was a legend. Here is how it started.

Dusty had practiced with his six shooter until his thumb and trigger finger had become calloused strong independent appendages. Unlike a lot of Western men, he practiced with both hands- he did not wear two guns for show. He could draw, aim, and shoot, just as well with either hand, a skill that would come in handy as his legend grew. Dusty also practiced with a rifle, and a

74

buffalo gun. Years later, a scout who worked briefly with Dusty during the Indian Wars saw Dusty bring down an Elk from almost a mile away.

"Shot right through the brain pan. " The man said: "At a mile. Could that boy shoot? I'd say so." Dusty had no idea how good he had gotten, he had no one to compare himself to. He just worked at being a little faster, shooting a little straighter, and hitting things that were moving, or farther away, as practice. Little did he know, he had passed the greatest shooters of the time in: speed, accuracy, and volley. Often, when unloading all six rounds into a target, Dusty's guns did not make a series of gunshots, just one long bang. Most times if he only got off two or three shots, witnesses only heard one "bang!" Still he had not killed anyone, nor had he been in a gunfight, or even a fist fight. Not yet. That would change…tomorrow.

Dusty got up on the range, folded his kit up, then fixed himself some coffee and beans. While they were cooking, he went out to the bushes to answer the call of nature. When he came back to camp, there they were. Three hombres. All of them ridden hard, and put away wet. Tough boys. Hard boys. Boys that had ridden both sides of the law. Fair to them did not matter. You lived another day, or you didn't. It was all the same to them. So it wasn't any concern of theirs, if this tenderfoot lived or died. He had supplies that they needed, so if he couldn't protect those supplies, why, they reckoned, they weren't meant to be his at all. They had already helped themselves to the welcome coffee, made just the way Western men liked it: hot, strong, and plenty. Dusty stepped out of the bramble, and fixed his belt. It was only then he noticed the three men.

"Mornin, boys."

"Howdy back at ya."

"What is it you boys want? I see you helped yourself to the coffee. That's okay, I can make more."

The three men glanced at each other. They had done this to stragglers and many a tenderfoot from Back East. They saw that he was wearing two guns, which was a dead give away that he probably couldn't use them. Nobody out West wore two guns, because they knew they would be challenged to see if those guns were for show. They also noted the pack horse filled with supplies. It is why they stopped. One man, two horses, one of them a pack horse, was a sure sign this boy was from Back East. Headed West with silly dreams of becoming a man, or a rancher, or starting a new life. Instead, that life was going to end right here, out on the range. In the open. In front of the last fire that boy would ever make. The men smiled at his naive bravado.

"We want a bit more than your coffee and beans, young fellow. " The tallest of the three pointed towards the horses and supplies. "We figure we shall just take the horses and supplies, and you can walk and think about what you did wrong. The next town ain't but thirty or so miles from here. Walking, you ought to be there by Sundown. " The three men laughed.

Just then a dust devil swooped by, stirring up the fire, sending little flames like fiery butterflies twenty feet into the air. It also covered William Henry Buckley with dust.

"Well, look at you boy! All covered with dust. Why it is a sign from the Bible: "...dust an unto dust you shall return." All the men laughed. "Dusty. We shall write that on your cross."

"You going to bury me then?"

"Well...Dusty. We being Civilized men, but in a hurry. Don't figure on burying you. The coyotes, and bears need to eat. But, we are Christians, so we will make you a marker. Every man should have at least a marker when he dies. Don't you think?"

"I didn't know that bit of Western Lore. But it is good to know. I don't have to bury you three, I just have to make a marker. Saves me time. Now that you told me where the town is."

The three men had no idea what this little dust mite meant. It should have been a clue that Dusty - as they named him, was not the lead bit afraid. He had left being afraid back East. The three men did not know that he had fought both a bear, and a mountain lion, and won. Nor did they know he had survived the coldest winter on record, by finding and living with a hibernating bear. No. Fear and Dusty had parted ways a long time ago. Even when his canoe took him and his supplies over a twenty foot waterfall, and 17 miles of rapids, he didn't panic, even though he damn near drowned. The beating he took on the rocks, would have killed most men. But he kept on. He had a dream, and that dream was in the West, and he wasn't stopping, nor would anybody stop him until he chased that dream and treed it.

The men had done this before. Braced a brave man with a gun. But there were three of them, and just one brave man. They followed their routine, it had never failed them before. One stayed put, the other two moved six feet away to either side. They knew that the other fella would now have to turn and choose a target, and by that time he would be dead. Riddled from the bullets of three guns. So they eased into their positions, in a sliding movement, a practiced movement, a well worn, oiled movement. Leaving Dusty facing one man, with two of them just on the edge of his periphial vision. He smiled. "Good thing I took geometry in school."

That comment was so out of place in the Western mind, so unexpected, so novel, that the two outriders looked over at the man in the middle as if to say: "What the heck does that mean?" The moment their eyes left Dusty, Dusty fired. "Baaaammmm!" One long bang. Six bullets, all of them finding their marks. The man in the middles hat flew off, followed shortly by most of the little brain he had. One eye fell on his cheek, hanging from a bloody cord. The man on the left felt like some horse or mule had kicked him in the chest, but it was just two bullets slamming into his heart, crushing his sternum, some ribs and shattering his heart. The man on the right fared no better. Because of the angle, the two bullets headed his way, ripped through his lung, liver, and heart, on the way to his spine, which severed all feeling from his lower body, if he had had any. Dead men don't feel.

There were no moans. No cries. Just a deathly stillness. Dusty's aim was such that there was no lingering death. The term "dropped dead" was an accurate one. A moment later outside the ring of the fire, Dusty heard a "giddyup" and the pounding of hoofs. A man on a horse , the fourth man, who was supposed to be the back up, the reserve, the fail safe, decided on the spot, to run. He saw that shootout. He knew he didn't stand a chance. So he jumped on his horse, with his gun out, figuring he would just fire some shots at the fellow still standing, so he would flinch or duck, then the man on the horse would be clear of that death machine. Riding hard for town. It would have worked too. If only Dusty had flinched , or ducked. He did not. He turned towards the racing horse, and in the dark, at a moving target, shot two more times, one shot from each gun.

One hit the pommel of the saddle, taking off the mans thumb and forefinger. The other bullet though, went in above his hip, and came out in the front right by his belly button. He was gut shot. It would take him more than two days to die. Long enough for him to get to Dry Gulch, and tell them about a man named Dusty. A short fella with red hair and deadly aim. The fastest gun in the West. They asked the dying man what the name of this shooter was.

"Dusty. At least that is what they called him just afore the shooting started. "

Later the same day the gut shot thief came into town, the Sheriff and a posse road out to the campsite. The animals hadn't quite chewed up all the bodies. The men lay where they had fallen. Guns still in their holsters. Bye each was a little wooden cross pounded into the ground. No name. No date. Just the words: Dead Thieves. The Sheriff and the Western Men in the posse, knew the three bodies by name. Bad men. Hard men. Fast with a gun men. They never got their guns out, and they had him in a crossfire. Out loud he said: "Dusty. There's a man you don't want to steal from." Heads nodded.

The legend…was born.

The man with the gun

By Kevin Hughes

He was tall. Lanky. Long. Slim.

He was quiet too.

He was as independent as the weather, and just as unpredictable.

If leather was a personality, it would be him.

He was…the man with the gun.

Right now, that gun was out.

Oh, nobody saw the gun come out of his holster.

One minute he was calm, the next he was just as calm, except, now, well, now he held a gun in his hand.

The man facing him, had guns. Two to be exact.

He meant to draw them both. He never got the chance.

He wasn't the man with guns out, merely the man that had guns.

As he looked down the barrel of the gun, in the hand of the man with the gun; his life flashed before his eyes.

A good thing it only took a flash,he wasn't alive to think about his life... by the time the "bang" hit his ears.

It was only later, when they prepared the body for burial, that they discovered three bullets, not one. Witnesses only heard the one bang, not three.

The Undertaker fainted. The Sheriff trembled. Three. Three shots that sounded like one. Even more scary is this- they all went through the same hole.

The Sheriff, for the first time since he was ten years old, prayed.

The man with the gun was long gone by that time. He found that staying in town after killing a man, meant killing more men. He did not like killing men. At least not men who were only trying for bragging rights. Many times the man with the gun, was the first to back down, apologize, or even walk away. Once. The second time was your choice, not his. You paid the price of wanting to know: "Is he really that fast? Is he really that strong? Is he really that quick. He knew the answer: "Yes." You did not, and you died finding out.

Lots of gunslingers (they called them "Shooters" in the Old West) got nicknames, and gloried in their short fancy lives. Briefly they reigned as the fastest gun in the West, or the Deadliest man in Tombstone, until some kid named Billy, Jessie, Earp, Hardin, or even Bat...became the newest legend. You have to be dead to be a legend. The man with the gun never picked up a name. He never bragged. He never paraded his skills. He never gave his name. His legend was a living one. Because you never knew his name. You just knew, you were standing here...and over there, stood the man with the gun. It was the last thing you would ever know.

Part 2

The door burst open. Glass. Wood. A doorknob. Then...a body. Bloody, Broken, already dead... as it flew through what was left of the frame.

Inside, men stood, or half squatted in fear. It was a single punch. One punch. A sound like bad melons hitting a rock. 220 pounds of what used to be a man, with what was left of what used to be a face, exploded through the door.

From outside it looked like an explosion threw a body through the door. From inside, where men stood in awe. Where the stink of fear filled the air, like old socks on wet feet. It didn't look possible. For years, the men who were there, would have trouble sleeping.

Not one of them, even though they were men of the Wild West, cut from solid rock and weathered by hard times, men who had braved winter with no more than leather to eat, would have considered themselves as tough as that man. One insult. One fist. One punch. One second. One death. It was over.

That it is all it took for the Man with a gun, to send another a soul on its last journey. He did it without a gun. They don't give notches out for fists. If they did, his would be covered like scars. The Man with a gun turned back to his drink. Someone would clean it up. Someone always did.

The Man with a gun decided to stay that night. He was tired. There was a hotel. At least for tonight, he was safe in town. The man he hit, had bullied the town for months. No one strong enough, brave enough...or maybe stupid enough to cross him. Until. The Man with a gun ordered a drink, and the bully boy put a cigar out in it.

The Man with a gun, was reasonable: "Pay for that drink. And buy me one without your cigar in it and we will walk away friends." The Man with a gun, turned back to the bar. The bully boy grabbed the Man with a gun by the shoulder, turning him to land a sucker punch, as he had to so many other drifters and farmers. His arm was still cocked to throw a punch when the Man with a gun's fist hit his face. Bones, vertebrae, teeth, and the will to live, all broke with that one punch. No. No one was going to bother the Man with a gun tonight.

Tomorrow? Well, tomorrow Is another day.

An Empty Holster

By Josh Wilkinson

I rode into town on the back of a mule. Maybe stumbled is a more appropriate word. Dust kicked up, floating softly down with every step it took. I was parched, dry, in a daze that only comes from the dry desert wind. Both my beast of burden and I were exhausted. Likely I couldn't have made it without the appearance of the mule. It was my third day of wandering; my first day after my canteen had gone dry. I had nearly collapsed, but then I saw it, ears perked up, staring at me, grey body trembling. It seemed wary of me, and rightly so, a man in my condition at that point is known to do anything. Still, I was so grateful to its appearance that I would have cried if I'd had any water left in me; it was fully saddled, and had a half-full canteen of water. I don't know where it came from, likely from a victim of outlaws, or the like. All I knew at that moment though, was that both me, and the animal, were the only way the other was going to survive.

We came into town sometime after noon. My hat was gone, I had lost it sometime out there, but I don't remember when. What I mostly remember is the burning sensation, the scorching of the body and the mind. I focused on nothing but satisfying my thirst. I slid off the back of the mule and tied it up, focusing all my energy on making it through the doors of what appeared to be the saloon.

The room was moderately crowded, but not as much as some of the others I'd seen. No one was at the counter. Several men sat around a table playing cards, three others watching. One man sat in the corner, seemingly sleeping with his brim down over his eyes. I walked to the counter, resting all my weight on the dark stained oak. The bartender looked me over, appraising my unshaven beard, dusty clothing, and empty holster.

"New in town?" He asked. I glanced up, nodded.

"What can I get you?"

"Start with water," I said quietly, hoarsely. He raised his eyebrows as he turned and entered a room behind the counter, returning with a full canteen. I drank it all in one swig.

"Can I get anything else for you?" he asked as I finished the canteen.

"You have a general store?"

"We do, but I probably have what you need down in the back. What do you need?"

I motioned to a large black hat sitting in the back of the room. It had a leather band around it, with a few beads around the band. "I'll have the hat."

He set it on the counter, and apparently realizing my current situation, began to question me. "You have the money for this?"

I reached into my pocket, pulling out a small sack. I plopped it down on the counter. "One of these should do." He undid the knot around the mouth and poured the contents into his hand. The bag was filled with twenty-five gold coins. He examined a few of them.

"These look fresh minted," he said, looking up at me, his voice somewhat cautious.

I looked at him, my eyes somewhat challenging. "Do they?" I asked.

One of the men playing cards stood up. He was tall, with broad shoulders, and had a large moustache that reached past the corners of his mouth. "You have a name?" he asked.

"Used to," I muttered as I took a sip from my drink.

He looked at me sternly as he exhaled from his nose. "Do you want to tell me where you got that money, or am I going to have to confiscate it?"

"You're welcome to try," I spoke, turning to face him. He just laughed.

"You're not even carrying a gun!"

The supposedly sleeping man in the corner spoke. "Let him be, Sam. Can't you tell this man's been through a lot lately?"

Sam grit his teeth. "Stay out of this Mathew. I don't need your interfering sentiments."

Mathew stood up and advanced until he stood before Sam. "So you've had a couple rough games. Don't take it out on this poor traveler here. Taking money from a defenseless man is low, even for you. Besides," he said gesturing to the card table, "you know better than to play cards with Mike Johnson."

Sam growled softly, and backed off. He nodded towards me. "Get him out of my sight!"

Mathew nodded, and put his arm on my shoulder. "Come on, let's go."

We strode out of the saloon, silently walking side by side until we reached his horse. It was tied up next to the mule. Finally, I spoke.

"Listen, I really didn't take that money. I don't know who had it before me, but I just found it. I'm not a thief."

He stopped walking, then nodded. "I believe you."

I have to admit, I was a little surprised.

"Why?"

He just smiled at me. "You don't look the type."

I contemplated this as he mounted his horse. Suddenly, he wheeled around. "By the way, I forgot to ask your name."

I thought of the name scratched into the canteen I was holding, the name that had spent days on my mind, the one thing that occupied my thoughts other than my own survival.

"Call me Chuck." I said. "Chuck Nolan."

I spent the next few weeks getting to know Mathew Callahan and his family. They lived on a ranch several miles from the town, a property that he had acquired through, "a small string of good fortunes." It was a large, sprawling property, filled with plenty of range, as well as a canyon to the north side, with a natural spring way back into it.

He hadn't always lived here, he told me one day. Years ago, he had been a lawman, a ranger in fact, until he left one day. When questioned he simply stated, "Personal reasons. Some have a taste for it, but I discovered I didn't." He looked down at my holster, still empty. "You ought to go into town with your first pay, Chuck, and buy you a new gun."

I shook my head. "No, it came into this town empty, and that's how it'll stay."

"Why's that?"

I patted the holster. "A reminder." He nodded his head, and didn't press it further. Mathew was good that way. He never pushed me to reveal more about myself than I wished, which was a quality rarely found in people.

I sold the mule. My beast of burden had served its purpose, and I saw no further need for it. I took the small supplies that I had found with it, and brought it to Mathew's home. He decided to keep me on as a hand, and for that I was grateful to him. It was a peaceful life, or more peaceful than the life I had lived before. I began to feel hope, an emotion I hadn't felt in a longer while than I cared to admit. But with that hope, came the insidious twinge of fear, that sensation that admittedly made the hair on the back of my neck stand on end, and caused the beginnings of doubt.

It was late August when Mathew rode into town. "Morning Mathew!" a few called. He tipped his hat as he rode towards the general store. It was early in the morning; the sun had yet to rise. The wind blew softly, slowly, carrying the soft dust with it. Mathew dismounted, as Zeke Johnson, owner of the general store, walked towards him.

"Morning Mathew!" he said cheerfully. "Come on in, and have yourself some coffee!"

"Much obliged," Mathew spoke gratefully.

Just as they were about to pass through the door, Mathew stopped. He listened carefully. The wind had died down, but there was a low rumbling in the distance, steadily growing louder by the second. A large cloud of dust grew larger in the distance, traveling west towards the town. As it came closer, the sound became more distinct: the rumbling of hooves, and the yells and shouts of men. Their dark shapes became clear against the cloud of dust; thirteen to twenty riders, headed at a hard pace towards the town. Mathew and Zeke watched with growing concern.

"Zeke," Mathew said. "Grab your rifle." Zeke nodded and ducked into the shop, reappearing quickly with his gun.

The riders moved in, there were six of them, bringing along with them a cloud of dust. It swept across the town and dispersed as the apparent leader stopped his horse, the other riders following suite.

"Whoa!" the lead rider shouted, his horse rearing up, then coming back down. Mathew froze as the rider's face turned his way; it was a face he had seen before, a voice he had heard, a visage he thought he'd be a witness to again.

The recognition was mutual. "Mathew Callahan!" the rider spoke, spitting into the ground. The rider was tall, his face appearing somewhat gaunt. He wore a large black hat, and a grey duster. His haggard face suddenly transformed entirely as he smiled, giving a somewhat roguish look, and revealing a gold tooth.

"What are you doing here Clyde?" Mathew questioned.

Clyde continued smiling, but did not dismount. He maneuvered his horse so that he stood directly above Mathew. He spoke. "We ran into some trouble a few towns back; one of the boys jumped a man at night, only to discover he was a ranger.

We've been on the run for a few days, but we can't go any farther." Clyde looked around the open street. He looked back at Mathew, speaking again. "This looks like as good a place as any for a last stand."

Mathew grit his teeth. "No Clyde. Get out of here. I don't want to have to do to you what I did to your brother."

Clyde frowned, looking at him with disdain. "Adam was a fool. He had the full support of dozens, but you call him out, and he goes alone, like he had to protect someone! No Mathew, you may be a good shot, but you're no Charlie Davis, not with my men around. Besides," he continued, "I heard you're not even a lawman anymore."

Mathew nodded at Zeke, almost imperceptibly, but a man in the posse was watching. As Mathew went for his holster, the man drew and fired. Mathew fell back, clutching his right arm. By this time, all the men in the posse were armed, many dismounted. Shocked, Zeke grabbed Mathew, helping him up as they ran through the doors of the store, quickly shutting it behind them and bolting it.

"We've got to get out to the stables," Zeke said, but Mathew just shook his head, cringing, and still clutching his arm.

"We won't make it, not unless there's something out there to distract them," He managed to speak through clenched teeth. The riders were pounding on the door, the timbers beginning to crack. Suddenly, a shot rang out. One of the riders, still mounted, fell off his horse. Clyde wheeled around to the direction of the shot, his pistol drawn. A man, the source of the shot, stood on a balcony from the hotel. He ran to the edge of the balcony, and barely pausing, jumped back into the alley next to the hotel. He landed on his horse, waiting in the alley, and let his steed come blasting out of the alley at a full gallop, heading out of the town at a remarkable speed. The riders fired wildly, but he was already out of range. Clyde swore softly, as one of the riders ran back up to him.

"That man was the sheriff. Name's Sam. Should we head after him?"

Clyde paused, staring at the east where the sun was beginning to rise over the desert. He shook his head. "No. We've got bigger things to worry about." He walked over to the store, where the door barely hung on to its hinges. Giving it a solid kick, it fell down. The store was empty.

"Gone," he said softly.

The sun had just begun to rise when Sam came riding in. I had been up early working, but hadn't had breakfast, and was heading to do so when he came riding in. He pulled up his horse directly in front of the house. And sat there in front of me, still clutching the reigns, his hands trembling.

"Can I help you, Sam?"

He looked at me a minute, dismounted, and then quickly explained the events that had taken place. Finally, he said, "I need your help."

"How?" I asked.

"I need you to help me take out Clyde."

I just shook my head. "You know I don't carry a gun. Of all people, why did you ask me?"

"Because," he said, "You're Charlie Davis."

I started. "Where did you-"

He interrupted me with a hand, giving a somewhat grim smile. "I told you," he said, "You matched a couple descriptions."

I stared at the ground a minute, silently. "Sam, I want to help. But I just can't- not with this, not anymore."

"Why? You had no trouble at Sonora, or down in El Paso."

"That was before…" I drifted off, falling into a silence. It was quiet a minute, until finally he spoke.

"Well, either way, I'm going after him, with or without your help." Sam mounted back onto his horse. "By the way," he said, "You might want to know that Mathew got shot." He started his horse off in a trot towards the town. He turned around and shouted, "Might give you something to think about!"

I stared off, my mind deep in thought. I knew it was bound to happen eventually, it always did. I was good for a while, stayed out of trouble, but it somehow always found me. It always started the same; some fool who wanted the reputation for killing Charlie Davis. It always ended the same way too. It was the same process that had led me to flee into the desert. And I had to do it again, pick up and go. I turned, preparing to leave.

A small thought pierced my mind. This is different than before. I paused. Maybe it was different. An idea began to form. Maybe there was a way for me to fix this mess, and still not leave the destruction that usually followed in my wake. I ran into the house, searching for a small bag. I felt around for an object, and feeling cold metal, I closed my hand around it. This could work! Grabbing it, I turned and rushed out the door, making my way to my horse, and began heading towards town.

I entered into town a short while later. The sun had risen higher in the sky, but the town was dead silent. In the street, two men faced each other, a short distance apart. One was Sam, the other I imagined being the man that Sam had described to me as Clyde. A grim expression was over both their faces, hands near their holsters.

I rode in, thundering, giving a loud shout. "Hold!"

They both veered in my direction, drawing their revolvers. Sam had a surprised look on his face. "Charlie?" he asked.

Clyde just looked at me. "Now who in the-"

I interrupted him. "Names Charlie Davis. Which one of you goes by the name of Clyde?"

Clyde started. "Ch- Charlie Davis?"

I looked at him. "Would you be Clyde?"

He recomposed himself. "I would. What do you want?"

"I need you to leave."

He laughed nervously. "You can't make me do that, you're just one man!"

I gave him a hard stare. He swallowed hard.

I shrugged. "Maybe I can't. More likely I can." All was silent for a moment, until I spoke again.

"Now, supposing I feel in a good mood today, I might just give you a chance to save yourself."

He looked puzzled. "What do you mean?"

I smiled, and dismounted. "You see that gas light over there?" I asked, pointing. It was the only one the town had.

He nodded skeptically.

"We're going to have a little contest. We both take a turn aiming and firing at that lamp over there. If you hit it, and I don't, you can stay, do with the town what you want. If we both hit it, you leave, no questions asked, and don't come back. But, if I hit it, and you don't..." I gave him another stare; he seemed to understand my meaning.

"Alright," He said shrugging uneasily.

I made a gesture. "After you."

He stepped forward, as he pointed his pistol, and then lowered it. "Just a minute," He said. "We need to switch guns. You made the Challenge. Plus, you're Charlie Davis; your gun is obviously better than mine."

I shrugged. "Fine by me."

He took it from my hand, and stepping forward, aiming carefully, he fired. It was a miss. He began to sweat profusely.

Taking the gun I had switched with Clyde, I repeated the process he had gone through. Releasing a breath, I fired.

Crash. There was a sound of shattering glass; my bullet had met its target. Clyde collapsed to his knees. "Please Charlie! Don't- I didn't-"

"Stand up Clyde, you lost!" I shouted.

A look of rage filled his face. He sprang to his feet, and fired my pistol at me. I fell backwards to the ground clutching my chest.

Suddenly from two opposing alleyways ran Mathew and Zeke, each aiming a gun at Clyde. Sam covered Clyde's men. "Drop it Clyde, hands up!" Mathew shouted, his one arm bandaged.

Clyde dropped his weapon, and Sam rounded him and his men up. Mathew, Sam, and Zeke came over to look at me. "Chuck?" Mathew said softly, bending over me.

I sprang to my feet. "Don't worry about me, I'm fine."

Sam looked confused. "But, how did-"

I walked over and picked up the revolver Clyde had used, and popped it open showing the contents in the chamber. "It was filled with blanks," I said.

Sam looked relieved. "Whew, for a second I was worried you were risking the town on your accuracy!"

"Well, that probably wouldn't have been much of a problem, it was his accuracy I was worried about. Besides, I knew he was likely to try a stunt like he just did."

Zeke clapped me on the back, and I shook Sam's hand. It was a warm, friendly shake. From then on, I always considered him to be a friend. As we walked, Mathew turned to me, and asked, "So, where did you get those blanks?"

I found them in the saddle of that mule. Figured it must have belonged to an actor previously."

"You gonna keep it?"

"Sure thing. Right where it belongs." I patted my holster, and we started for home.

Bad Medicine

By Andy Adams

The evening before the Cherokee Strip was thrown open for settlement, a number of old timers met in the little town of Hennessey, Oklahoma.

On the next day the Strip would pass from us and our employers, the cowmen. Some of the boys had spent from five to fifteen years on this range. But we realized that we had come to the parting of the ways.

This was not the first time that the government had taken a hand in cattle matters. Some of us in former days had moved cattle at the command of negro soldiers, with wintry winds howling an accompaniment.

The cowman was never a government favorite. If the Indian wards of the nation had a few million acres of idle land, "Let it lie idle," said the guardian. Some of these civilized tribes maintained a fine system of public schools from the rental of unoccupied lands. Nations, like men, revive the fable of the dog and the ox. But the guardian was supreme--the cowman went. This was not unexpected to most of us. Still, this country was a home to us. It mattered little if our names were on the pay-roll or not, it clothed and fed us.

We were seated around a table in the rear of a saloon talking of the morrow. The place was run by a former cowboy. It therefore became a rendezvous for the craft. Most of us had made up our minds to quit cattle for good and take claims.

"Before I take a claim," said Tom Roll, "I'll go to Minnesota and peon myself to some Swede farmer for my keep the balance of my life. Making hay and plowing fire guards the last few years have given me all the taste of farming that I want. I'm going to Montana in the spring."

"Why don't you go this winter? Is your underwear too light?" asked Ace Gee. "Now, I'm going to make a farewell play," continued Ace. "I'm going to take a claim, and before I file on it, sell my rights, go back to old Van Zandt County, Texas, this winter, rear up my feet, and tell it to them scarey. That's where all my folks live."

"Well, for a winter's stake," chimed in Joe Box, "Ace's scheme is all right. We can get five hundred dollars out of a claim for simply staking it, and we know some good ones. That sized roll ought to winter a man with modest tastes."

"You didn't know that I just came from Montana, did you, Tom?" asked Ace. "I can tell you more about that country than you want to know. I've been up the trail this year; delivered our cattle on the Yellowstone, where the outfit I worked for has a northern range. When I remember this summer's work, I sometimes think that I will burn my saddle and never turn or look a cow in the face again, nor ride anything but a plow mule and that bareback.

101

"The people I was working for have a range in Tom Green County, Texas, and another one in Montana. They send their young steers north to mature--good idea, too!--but they are not cowmen like the ones we know. They made their money in the East in a patent medicine--got scads of it, too. But that's no argument that they know anything about a cow. They have a board of directors--it is one of those cattle companies. Looks like they started in the cattle business to give their income a healthy outlet from the medicine branch. They operate on similar principles as those soap factory people did here in the Strip a few years ago. About the time they learn the business they go broke and retire.

"Our boss this summer was some relation to the wife of some of the medicine people Down East. As they had no use for him back there, they sent him out to the ranch, where he would be useful.

"We started north with the grass. Had thirty-three hundred head of twos and threes, with a fair string of saddle stock. They run the same brand on both ranges--the broken arrow. You never saw a cow-boss have so much trouble; a married woman wasn't a circumstance to him, fretting and sweating continually. This was his first trip over the trail, but the boys were a big improvement on the boss, as we had a good outfit of men along. My idea of a good cow-boss is a man that doesn't boss any; just hires a first-class outfit of men, and then there is no bossing to do.

"We had to keep well to the west getting out of Texas; kept to the west of Buffalo Gap. From there to Tepee City is a dry, barren country. To get water for a herd the size of ours was some trouble. This new medicine man got badly worried several times. He used his draft book freely, buying water for the cattle while crossing this stretch of desert; the natives all through there considered him the softest snap they had met in years. Several times we were without water for the stock two whole days. That makes cattle hard to hold at night. They want to get up and prowl--it makes them feverish, and then's when they are ripe for a stampede. We had several bobles crossing that strip of country; nothing bad, just jump and run a mile or so, and then mill until daylight. Then our boss would get great action on himself and ride a horse until the animal would give out--sick, he called it. After the first little run we had, it took him half the next day to count them; then he couldn't believe his own figures.

"A Val Verde County lad who counted with him said they were all right--not a hoof shy. But the medicine man's opinion was the reverse. At this the Val Verde boy got on the prod slightly, and expressed himself, saying, 'Why don't you have two of the other boys count them? You can't come within a hundred of me, or yourself either, for that matter. I can pick out two men, and if they differ five head, it'll be a surprise to me. The way the boys have brought the cattle by us, any man that can't count this herd and not have his own figures differ more than a hundred had better quit riding, get himself some sandals, and a job herding sheep. Let me give you this pointer: if you are not anxious to have last night's fun over again, you'd better quit counting and get this herd full of grass and water before night, or you will be cattle shy as sure as hell's hot.'

"'When I ask you for an opinion,' answered the foreman, somewhat indignant, 'such remarks will be in order. Until then you may keep your remarks to yourself.'

"'That will suit me all right, old sport,' retorted Val Verde; 'and when you want any one to help you count your fat cattle, get some of the other boys--one that'll let you doubt his count as you have mine, and if he admires you for it, cut my wages in two.'

"After the two had been sparring with each other some little time, another of the boys ventured the advice that it would be easy to count the animals as they came out of the water; so the order went forward to let them hit the trail for the first water. We made a fine stream, watering early in the afternoon. As they grazed out from the creek we fed them through between two of the boys. The count showed no cattle short. In fact, the Val Verde boy's count was confirmed. It was then that our medicine man played his cards wrong. He still insisted that we were cattle out, thus queering himself with his men. He was gradually getting into a lone minority, though he didn't have sense enough to realize it. He would even fight with and curse his horses to impress us with his authority. Very little attention was paid to him after this, and as grass and water improved right along nothing of interest happened.

"While crossing 'No-Man's-Land' a month later,--I was on herd myself at the time, a bright moonlight night,--they jumped like a cat shot with No. 8's, and quit the bed-ground instanter. There were three of us on guard at the time, and before the other boys could get out of their blankets and into their saddles the herd had

104

gotten well under headway. Even when the others came to our assistance, it took us some time to quiet them down. As this scare came during last guard, daylight was on us before they had quit milling, and we were three miles from the wagon. As we drifted them back towards camp, for fear that something might have gotten away, most of the boys scoured the country for miles about, but without reward. When all had returned to camp, had breakfasted, and changed horses, the counting act was ordered by Mr. Medicine. Our foreman naturally felt that he would have to take a hand in this count, evidently forgetting his last experience in that line. He was surprised, when he asked one of the boys to help him, by receiving a flat refusal.

"'Why won't you count with me?' he demanded.

"'Because you don't possess common cow sense enough, nor is the crude material in you to make a cow-hand. You found fault with the men the last count we had, and I don't propose to please you by giving you a chance to find fault with me. That's why I won't count with you.'

"'Don't you know, sir, that I'm in authority here?' retorted the foreman.

"'Well, if you are, no one seems to respect your authority, as you're pleased to call it, and I don't know of any reason why I should. You have plenty of men here who can count them correctly. I'll count them with any man in the outfit but yourself.'

"'Our company sent me as their representative with this herd,' replied the foreman, 'while you have the insolence to disregard my orders. I'll discharge you the first moment I can get a man to take your place.'

"'Oh, that'll be all right,' answered the lad, as the foreman rode away. He then tackled me, but I acted foolish, 'fessing up that I couldn't count a hundred. Finally he rode around to a quiet little fellow, with pox-marks on his face, who always rode on the point, kept his horses fatter than anybody, rode a San Jose saddle, and was called Californy. The boss asked him to help him count the herd.

"'Now look here, boss,' said Californy, 'I'll pick one of the boys to help me, and we'll count the cattle to within a few head. Won't that satisfy you?'

"'No, sir, it won't. What's got into you boys?' questioned the foreman.

"'There's nothing the matter with the boys, but the cattle business has gone to the dogs when a valuable herd like this will be trusted to cross a country for two thousand miles in the hands of a man like yourself. You have men that will pull you through if you'll only let them,' said the point-rider, his voice mild and kind as though he were speaking to a child.

"'You're just like the rest of them!' roared the boss. 'Want to act contrary! Now let me say to you that you'll help me to count these

106

cattle or I'll discharge, unhorse, and leave you afoot here in this country! I'll make an example of you as a warning to others.'

"'It's strange that I should be signaled out as an object of your wrath and displeasure,' said Californy. 'Besides, if I were you, I wouldn't make any examples as you were thinking of doing. When you talk of making an example of me as a warning to others,' said the pox-marked lad, as he reached over, taking the reins of the foreman's horse firmly in his hand, 'you're a simpering idiot for entertaining the idea, and a cowardly bluffer for mentioning it. When you talk of unhorsing and leaving me here afoot in a country a thousand miles from nowhere, you don't know what that means, but there's no danger of your doing it. I feel easy on that point. But I'm sorry to see you make such a fool of yourself. Now, you may think for a moment that I'm afraid of that ivory-handled gun you wear, but I'm not. Men wear them on the range, not so much to emphasize their demands with, as you might think. If it were me, I'd throw it in the wagon; it may get you into trouble. One thing certain, if you ever so much as lay your hand on it, when you are making threats as you have done to-day, I'll build a fire in your face that you can read the San Francisco "Examiner" by at midnight. You'll have to revise your ideas a trifle; in fact, change your tactics. You're off your reservation bigger than a wolf, when you try to run things by force. There's lots better ways. Don't try and make talk stick for actions, nor use any prelude to the real play you wish to make. Unroll your little game with the real thing. You can't throw alkaline dust in my eyes and tell me it's snowing. I'm sorry to have to tell you all this, though I have noticed that you needed it for a long time.'

"As he released his grip on the bridle reins, he continued, 'Now ride back to the wagon, throw off that gun, tell some of the boys to take a man and count these cattle, and it will be done better than if you helped.'

"'Must I continue to listen to these insults on every hand?' hissed the medicine man, livid with rage.

"'First remove the cause before you apply the remedy; that's in your line,' answered Californy. 'Besides, what are you going to do about it? You don't seem to be gifted with enough cow-sense to even use a modified amount of policy in your every-day affairs,' said he, as he rode away to avoid hearing his answer.

"Several of us, who were near enough to hear this dressing-down of the boss at Californy's hands, rode up to offer our congratulations, when we noticed that old Bad Medicine had gotten a stand on one of the boys called 'Pink.' After leaving him, he continued his ride towards the wagon. Pink soon joined us, a broad smile playing over his homely florid countenance.

"'Some of you boys must have given him a heavy dose for so early in the morning,' said Pink, 'for he ordered me to have the cattle counted, and report to him at the wagon. Acted like he didn't aim to do the trick himself. Now, as I'm foreman,' continued Pink, 'I want you two point-men to go up to the first little rise of ground, and we'll put the cattle through between you.

I want a close count, understand. You're working under a boss now that will shove you through hell itself. So if you miss them over a hundred, I'll speak to the management, and see if I can't have your wages raised, or have you made a foreman or something with big wages and nothing to do.'

"The point-men smiled at Pink's orders, and one asked, 'Are you ready now?'

"'All set,' responded Pink. 'Let the fiddlers cut loose.'

"Well, we lined them up and got them strung out in shape to count, and our point-men picking out a favorite rise, we lined them through between our counters. We fed them through, and as regularly as a watch you could hear Californy call out to his pardner 'tally!' Alternately they would sing out this check on the even hundred head, slipping a knot on their tally string to keep the hundreds. It took a full half hour to put them through, and when the rear guard of crips and dogies passed this impromptu review, we all waited patiently for the verdict. Our counters rode together, and Californy, leaning over on the pommel of his saddle, said to his pardner, 'What you got?'

"'Thirty-three six,' was the answer.

"'Why, you can't count a little bit,' said Californy. 'I got thirty-three seven. How does the count suit you, boss?'

"'Easy suited, gents,' said Pink. 'But I'm surprised to find such good men with a common cow herd. I must try and have you appointed by the government on this commission that's to investigate Texas fever. You're altogether too accomplished for such a common calling as claims you at present.'

"Turning to the rest of us, he said, 'Throw your cattle on the trail, you vulgar peons, while I ride back to order forward my wagon and saddle stock. By rights, I ought to have one of those centre fire cigars to smoke, to set off my authority properly on this occasion.'

"He jogged back to the wagon and satisfied the dethroned medicine man that the cattle were there to a hoof. We soon saw the saddle horses following, and an hour afterward Pink and the foreman rode by us, big as fat cattle-buyers from Kansas City, not even knowing any one, so absorbed in their conversation were they; rode on by and up the trail, looking out for grass and water.

"It was over two weeks afterward when Pink said to us, 'When we strike the Santa Fe Railway, I may advise my man to take a needed rest for a few weeks in some of the mountain resorts. I hope you all noticed how worried he looks, and, to my judgment, he seems to be losing flesh. I don't like to suggest anything, but the day before we reach the railroad, I think a day's curlew shooting in the sand hills along the Arkansas River might please his highness. In case he'll go with me, if I don't lose him, I'll never come back to this herd. It won't hurt him any to sleep out one night with the dry cattle.'

"Sure enough, the day before we crossed that road, somewhere near the Colorado state line, Pink and Bad Medicine left camp early in the morning for a curlew hunt in the sand hills.

Fortunately it was a foggy morning, and within half an hour the two were out of sight of camp and herd. As Pink had outlined the plans, everything was understood. We were encamped on a nice stream, and instead of trailing along with the herd, lay over for that day. Night came and our hunters failed to return, and the next morning we trailed forward towards the Arkansas River. Just as we went into camp at noon, two horsemen loomed up in sight coming down the trail from above. Every rascal of us knew who they were, and when the two rode up, Pink grew very angry and demanded to know why we had failed to reach the river the day before.

"The horse wrangler, a fellow named Joe George, had been properly coached, and stepping forward, volunteered this excuse: 'You all didn't know it when you left camp yesterday morning that we were out the wagon team and nearly half the saddle horses. Well, we were. And what's more, less than a mile below on the creek was an abandoned Indian camp. I wasn't going to be left behind with the cook to look for the missing stock, and told the _segundo_ so. We divided into squads of three or four men each and went out and looked up the horses, but it was after six o'clock before we trailed them down and got the missing animals. If anybody thinks I'm going to stay behind to look for missing stock in a country full of lurking Indians--well, they simply don't know me.'

"The scheme worked all right. On reaching the railroad the next morning, Bad Medicine authorized Pink to take the herd to Ogalalla on the Platte, while he took a train for Denver. Around the camp-fire that night, Pink gave us his experience in losing Mr. Medicine. 'Oh, I lost him late enough in the day so he couldn't reach any shelter for the night,' said Pink. 'At noon, when the sun was straight overhead, I sounded him as to directions and found that he didn't know straight up or east from west. After giving him the slip, I kept an eye on him among the sand hills, at the distance of a mile or so, until he gave up and unsaddled at dusk. The next morning when I overtook him, I pretended to be trailing him up, and I threw enough joy into my rapture over finding him, that he never doubted my sincerity.'

"On reaching Ogalalla, a man from Montana put in an appearance in company with poor old Medicine, and as they did business strictly with Pink, we were left out of the grave and owly council of medicine men. Well, the upshot of the whole matter was that Pink was put in charge of the herd, and a better foreman I never worked under. We reached the company's Yellowstone range early in the fall, counted over and bade our dogies good-by, and rode into headquarters. That night I talked with the regular men on the ranch, and it was there that I found out that a first-class cowhand could get in four months' haying in the summer and the same feeding it out in the winter. But don't you forget it, she's a cow country all right. I always was such a poor hand afoot that I passed up that country, and here I am a 'boomer.'"

"Well, boom if you want," said Tom Roll, "but do you all remember what the governor of North Carolina said to the governor of South Carolina?"

"It is quite a long time between drinks," remarked Joe, rising, "but I didn't want to interrupt Ace."

As we lined up at the bar, Ace held up a glass two thirds full, and looking at it in a meditative mood, remarked: "Isn't it funny how little of this stuff it takes to make a fellow feel rich! Why, four bits' worth under his belt, and the President of the United States can't hire him."

As we strolled out into the street, Joe inquired, "Ace, where will I see you after supper?"

"You will see me, not only after supper, but all during supper, sitting right beside you."

Sheriff, You Killed My Brother

By Ed DeRousse

"I hear Ned Buntline wants to put you in one of his books, Sheriff. How do you feel about that?"

"I don't particularly care for it. When he puts you in one of his books, unwanted things happen. And it is what's in those books, you are judged by."

"I don't understand. Don't you want to be famous, like Wild Bill?"

"Nope."

"I don't understand?"

"I am a tough lawman, and do have the real reputation to go with it. It's what I did to earn that reputation. It's not a made up reality some writer created in his own mind to help sell his books.."

"Sheriff, you do have a reputation of being a tough but just man. You carry that fancy Colt on your hip, but I've never seen you use it. Yet you are well known around here for your gun abilities. How many gunfights have you been in?"

"It's my reputation that makes not drawing my Colt much easier. I resolve issues without the use of gunplay. Innocent people run the risk of getting hurt whenever a gun is drawn. People believe me to be a superb gun handler. And that's Ok. It helps me maintain the peace around here."

"That didn't answer my question, Sheriff. Have you ever been on the street to meet a man face to face in showdown, like those characters in the Western books?"

"Son, perhaps, because of my reputation, I have never had to meet a man, face to face, on the street, in a showdown."

"It's almost Noon. Dirk Jackson's gonna be out there in the middle of that street in a few minutes. If you've not actually done that before, aren't you worried?"

"I have dealt with bad men before. Jackson read about himself in one of Buntline's books and is just trying to live up to his expectations. Buntline says he frequently meets the local lawman in the street to duel. Dirk's just some penny ante outlaw that's been luckier than most.

The thing is, though, Ned Buntline makes lots of money creating legends. Facts don't seem to be too important to him. Men met their demise because of Buntline's money making scheme.

I've read some of his novels and met some of his legends. I even incarcerated two or three of them without using my pistol.

Ned Buntline and other dime novel writers are the big problem in the West, not these make believe legends. It's the "code of the west" thing these writers created that puts me on the street today."

"Code of the west? What's that?"

"They're just a set of unwritten rules of survival all of the West supposedly lives by. The truth is, they don't exist, except in the minds of these writers from the East."

"With your reputation, how come you're not in one of his books?"

"I met Buntline long before I became a sheriff. He was beginning to create his legends back then and I watched his legends struggle to live up to what they were supposed to be. They had no choice. People were believing what was written about them.

Even back then I had a strong sense of right and wrong. My code was and still is the same as the men who wrote the words of the Bible. Those words don't seem to be what men like Buntline feel are words to sell by.

I felt strongly about using those words to help in the development of this new land. I had no desire to be a romanticized character in a dime novel. That would require me to live up to a different set of standards.

The West, in reality, is a hard and often unforgiving land. Most of us are just trying to survive.

Some of us, like the cowboy getting ready to face me now, find it easier or more thrilling to take. That makes him an abuser of God's word. There is nothing romantic about that."

"Sheriff, I'm out here in the street. You killed my brother! It's time for you to meet your maker!"

"That must be Jackson, Sheriff"

"It's time, son. It will be over soon."

"Dirk, we don't have to do this."

"Ya killed my brother!"

"It was him or me, Dirk."

"Doesn't matter, you killed my brother. It's your turn to die!"

"Dirk, we don't have to do this. There is another way."

"Yep! There is and you're still gonna die!"

I wonder, 'Will he actually draw his gun against me?'

Somehow, I know he will.

He has the reputation that tells me he will.

I feel no evil. I am not afraid of evil.

117

I will not draw first, but I will defend myself and this land I love.

"Sheriff, you killed my brother!"

His eyes tell me his intentions. I see his hand drop toward his gun.

Time slowed down............

I sense my hand reach for my gun.

His hand is already on the butt of his weapon and his thumb on the hammer.

I feel the handle of my Colt and my finger on the trigger. My hammer is already cocked.

Jackson's yelling something at me and yanking his gun out of his holster.

I see the barrel of his gun pointed at my chest.

Somehow mine is now pointed at his.

I see him squeeze the trigger, hear the roar of the gun, and see the black powder smoke bellowing from it.

I want to move to the right, but I can't until I fire. Will it be too late?

I hear my gun respond to my finger.

Time slowed down even more.

I see Jackson's bullet coming toward my chest.

I see a bullet leave my gun and its path is true.

I feel the sting of his bullet as it enters my chest. The sheer force of its entry into my body has made me lose my footing.

Jackson is falling toward the ground with a hole in his shirt where his heart would be.

I am convinced he breathes no more.

And, like my adversary, here I am, lying on my back.

I see the sun shining bright in the sky above me.

I'm burning up.

People are gathering around me.

I can't make them out.

I hear a soft feminine voice calling my name.

Could it be an Angel I hear?

"Sheriff, Sheriff,"

That voice sounds familar. Could it be?

"Honey, Honey, wake up! You're having a bad dream! Wake up Pete."

And suddenly, that soft voice I hear is that of my sweet wife.

The Clint Eastwood marathon, that old Ned Buntline Dime Novel I found a few days ago, and that late night meal really did a number on me.

Colorado

By Jon Foster

(Note that the author was 15 years old when he wrote this story.)

The train chugged into the Denver Station. The train was on its final leg of the New York to Denver Route. As the white-capped peaks of the mountains came into view, a man, clad in leather boots, walked to the front of the railroad car.

He was a younger man, about 25 years old, had brown hair and was quite tall and lean. But he had a muscular build. The hat he wore was dusty, well worn, and tan colored, and he wore a shirt that matched his eyes. His eyes were as blue as the Colorado sky. The young man also wore a pair of faded khaki-colored trousers. The gun-belt he wore around his waist was made of the finest cowhide. Yet it too was showing signs of wear. In the holster was a pair of Colt revolving handguns. He walked with a certain swagger in his step. His face was cool and confident. The young man had some stubble on his chin for a slightly beard-like look.

He walked around into the railcar where his horse was being held. The summer sun beat down upon his neck. He stopped to mop his brow, glad to be back. His friend was in New York, and he went there to visit him, now he was just returning and needed a rest. He mounted his chocolate colored stallion, rode into town, and checked into the nearest hotel for the night.

The young man awoke with a start. "Good Morning!" was said in an unfamiliar voice. Looking up, he saw a man sitting in his hotel room. This man was an older man, dressed in a suit, and he wore brand-new polished black shoes. The sun was just above the horizon.

"Hello." replied the younger man.

"You must be Jones."

"That's right"

"Good I need your help."

Why would this person need his help? Jones pondered. This older man was obviously rich. He could afford new shoes.

"Why me?" Jones asked. Couldn't he have hired any one else? He thought.

"Let me explain. Exactly ten days ago thieves stole all of the gold reserves from the Crescent City Bank. Jones, I'd like to hire you to investigate this bank robbery."

"Me? An investigator?" Jones sounded puzzled.

"Yes. You come highly recommended by Jeremiah Lewiston."

Well! Jones' old friend Jerry! Jerry was a hard man, but a loyal friend. He was also one of the most feared gunslingers in the West. Jones replied, still puzzled. "How do you know Jeremiah Lewiston?"

"Well, the mayor knows him personally…"

"The mayor?"

"Yes. The mayor of Crescent City."

"I've heard of Jeremiah Lewiston and I've also heard of Crescent City. But who are you?" Jones was still puzzled.

"I apologize for not introducing myself sooner. I am on the city council of Crescent City. I am the treasurer and I am also the mayor's personal advisor. My name is Benjamin Harris."

That would explain the new shoes, Jones thought.

Harris continued, "I will pay for your fare on the stagecoach, and you will be paid $25 a day to investigate the robbery of the Bank of Crescent City."

Jones considered this. Somehow he felt that he could not trust Harris. It seemed rather uncouth for him to come barging into his room without a prior introduction. Even though he had never met Harris till now, he felt as though there was something untrustworthy about wealthy and influential men. They always made him apprehensive. And also, he had never been a detective. Nevertheless, $25 a day was very good wages for 1879. He also wanted to see Jerry again. Contemplating it a bit more, he announced his decision.

"I accept!"

Five hours later, the stage rumbled into Crescent City. And as it did clouds started to build up, and a strong wind whistled.

"Well Jones, here we are." proclaimed Harris, inbetween claps of rolling thunder. Jones looked around. What he saw stunned him. Seven years ago, Jones had arrived in Crescent City on his first cattle drive from El Paso. Instead of going back to El Paso he stayed in Colorado. For years he went from town to town. Jones promoted justice and was the unofficial "protector" of Colorado. Wherever the bad guys were, Jones was there. His gunslinging earned him the nickname of "Colorado" Jones. His travels took him all throughout Colorado. Yet in the seven years that he had been gone from Crescent City, things had changed. They had changed a lot. Once a peaceful, busy, quiet little town, Crescent City was now the poorly maintained home of all of the outlaws in Colorado.

"How could Crescent City become so... so... corrupted?" Jones asked.

"Hard times, Mr. Jones. Hard times." Harris responded. "Looks like a storm is building. Let me take you down to visit the bank before you get wet."

"No. I am going to meet a friend. He lives near here. I'll ride over to his place. A little rain never hurt anybody. And you don't need to book me a hotel room. I have made arrangements."

"Very well." Harris sighed.

Jeremiah Lewiston stood on the front porch of his house. Rain was coming down in sheets. He stared into the big black storm clouds. 'Jerry' was in his mid-40's and still strong. He was wearing an old, tattered straw hat that showed his copper colored hair. The leather coat that Jeremiah wore was faded, but it served as a good raincoat, as the leather was still waterproof. He also wore a beard. His green eyes shone like big, green emeralds. Jerry looked down toward the path. It was still raining heavily. He saw that there was a man on a horse coming up the path. Could it be Colorado? No way. But sure enough there he was.

Colorado brought his horse to a halt. "Hey, old friend!"

"My, my! If it ain't Colorado Jones! Why don't you come on the porch? You look soaked. I'll make you some coffee."

"Thanks. I could use some coffee." Colorado dismounted and strolled onto the porch. Rain dripped from his wide-brimmed hat. "How've you been doing lately, Jerry?"

"Not too bad. You?"

"I'm good." stated Jones, apathetically.

"What's wrong Colorado?"

"You know about a bank robbery?"

"Come on inside. We need to talk." Jeremiah's voice sounded downhearted and listless.

Colorado sat down at the table. He took a nice, long sip of his piping hot coffee. It tasted so good to him. He stopped for a minute to listen to the rain hitting the roof, and then took another sip. Thunder rumbled in the distance. It had been a while since Jones last had a good cup of coffee.

"Now, why'd you ask about a bank robbery?" Jerry asked straightforwardly.

"Benjamin Harris…"

"Wait! Did you say Benjamin Harris?"

"Yes. I did."

"How do you know Benjamin Harris?"

"Why, I met him in Denver. He was the one who came to hire me to investigate the bank robbery I told you about."

"Benjamin Harris is the most crooked, reprehensible man I have ever met. Five years ago, he swindled me out of a city council seat. The town has been run down ever since. But anyway, about that bank robbery." Jerry took a deep breath. "Eleven days ago, $20,000 worth of fifty-dollar gold pieces, all of them fresh out of the mint, arrived in a wagon. It was heavily armed. That night in the local hotel the only detective in town was shot to death in the lobby. The next morning, all of the $20,000 was gone."

"Stolen?"

"Why else would it be missing?"

"Do you have any suspects?" Colorado sounded calm as ever.

"No, but I have always suspected that two-faced, treacherous crook Harris. My reason for my misgivings is that the day before the bank robbery Harris went out and bought himself some $100 shoes in Denver. When he came back, he bragged to everyone about his new shoes. Not even Harris is wealthy enough to buy $100 shoes."

Tense silence followed. Outside, more thunder boomed. For a few moments no one talked. Colorado took another sip of his coffee.

"What should I do?" Colorado asked assertively.

"Do what you were hired to do. Start by going down to the bank."

"Right."

"Listen, Colorado, you are the best gunman on either side of the Mississippi. Let those outlaws know you're not afraid. And make sure they do it your way. If they hired you, they must not know that you're Colorado Jones. The only reason Harris hired you is because I recommended you to the mayor."

"Thanks, Jerry. I owe you a lot." Colorado got up to leave. "By the way, you make great coffee."

The rain had ended when Colorado Jones stepped into the Crescent City Bank. He walked up to the counter.

"What can I do for you?" said the clerk.

"I am investigating the robbery of eleven days ago. Were there any witnesses?"

"Just one." The clerk stopped. "Jane! Come here, Jane!"

"Yes?"

"Jane, meet Mr., um…"

"Jones."

"Jane, meet Mr. Jones." The clerk went on. "He wants to know if you know anything about the bank robbery eleven days ago."

"I do know one thing. I could not take my eyes off of the robber's new shoes." said Jane, nonchalantly.

"What color were they?" said Jones, enthusiastically.

"Blacker than night. And all freshly polished, too."

Jones turned and walked out of the bank.

"What's that all about?" asked Jane, faintly.

"I don't rightly know." stated the clerk.

Jones came strolling out of the bank. Benjamin Harris was waiting for him.

"Well, did you find anything?" Benjamin Harris sounded uneasy.

"Nope."

"Oh."

"Well, I'm going down to the saloon." Jones said casually. "I need something to drink. You coming?"

"No. I need to meet someone."

"Very good. I'll be down there if you need me."

Benjamin Harris was edgy. He rode his chestnut colored horse down to his apartment. Waiting for him was a group of shady looking men. Harris spoke to the men. "Jones is on to us. I think he knows who stole the money from the Crescent City Bank. I'm sure he knows that it's us. Jeremiah Lewiston is on to us as well."

"Impossible! Even though I do know that Jeremiah has been onto us since day one, why would Jones be on to us?" declared the leader of the men.

"I am sure that Jeremiah knows Jones, and no, it's not impossible for Jones to be on to us. I did not know this when the mayor asked me to hire him, but Jones is the famed lawman Colorado Jones. Go down to the saloon. We need to get Jones off of our back at once. If Colorado says he's going back to Denver, let him be. At least he'll be out of the way in Denver."

"And if he's not going back to Denver?"

"Kill him."

Colorado gulped down another glass of sarsaparilla. "I'm leaving for Denver tomorrow." he told the bartender. "Tell Benjamin Harris to meet me at the stagecoach for Denver. Tell him to meet me there before dawn tomorrow."

"I sure will." replied the bartender, automatically. Jones went outside, mounted his horse, and rode hard for Jeremiah's ranch.

"You found WHAT?" Jeremiah Lewiston thundered. "A black scuff mark from new shoes. I also talked to a witness, and she says the man who robbed the bank had on polished, brand-new, shiny black shoes."

"No way! I knew Harris was a thief, but, this... this is very hard to believe!!"

"Do you know any one else who wears polished, black, brand-new shoes?"

"No. Only Benjamin Harris wears those kind of shoes." acknowledged Jeremiah. "You need to go back to Denver and round up some men so you can catch Harris."

"Sure thing, Jerry."

Colorado prepared to board the stagecoach back to Denver.

"Well, here's fifty dollars for your troubles!"

"Thanks, Harris."

Colorado got into the stagecoach. He needed to find some solid evidence. With wandering eyes Jones looked down at the gold piece in his hands. He stopped. Sitting in his hands was one of the stolen fifty-dollar gold pieces.

Harris was relieved. He finally had managed to shake that imprudent Jones fellow off of his tail. He had rewarded for him his two days' worth of work by paying him with one of the fifty-dollar gold pieces he had stolen from the bank. Even so, Harris was sure he had gotten away with it. He called his vigilantes together.

"Men! Congratulations on our victory! We're going down to the saloon to celebrate! I'll buy the drinks!"

Cheers and applause rose up from the gang. Suddenly, Colorado Jones, Jeremiah Lewiston, the county sheriff, and four other men walked up.

Colorado spoke first. "Having a party are we?"

131

"I thought you left town!" said Harris, incredulous.

BANG!!! A shot rang out from Harris' left. One of Jones' men fell dead. Harris mounted up, and rode hard. He heard horses follow him.

"Halt! You are under arrest!" The voice was that of Colorado Jones.

BANG!!! Another shot. This time the shot came from one of Colorado's Colt revolvers. Harris' horse stumbled and fell. He felt a pain in his side as he hit the ground. The last thing Benjamin Harris remembered seeing was the stone-cold faces of Colorado Jones and Jeremiah Lewiston.

Harris was arrested and his gang dispersed. He was convicted of forging documents (as a city treasurer) and theft. Harris was also charged with the mishandling of funds. Benjamin Harris was sentenced to 25 years in prison.

Two years later, Colorado Jones was elected mayor of Crescent City. Jeremiah Lewiston was appointed to city council. And Crescent City was once again the peaceful, affluent town it had once been.

Jones retired from law work once he was voted in as the mayor of Crescent City. But forever he will be known as the man called Colorado!

Tuck Jackson and The Carsons

By Shane Polley

(Note that Shane was 15 years old when he wrote this story.)

I, Tuck Jackson, was cornered and there wasn't any way I could get out. The Carson boys had me surrounded and were closing in. I had my six-shooter and my Winchester ready; they wouldn't get me without a fight. I never wanted a fight but I got myself a war.

In Houston a few years back I met up with Jesse Carson while getting a drink at the saloon. Carson, who was totally drunk, figured himself fast with a pistol, and he thought he'd make it known by killing me. He was looking for a fight. Carson walked over to me and said flatly, "I don't like you!" I could hardly suppress a grin, so I smiled and replied, "I don't cotton to you either!" "I aim to kill you," said Carson. "You can try, but you might get killed in the process," I said in reply. Silence filled the room. Carson went for his gun, but he was a might too slow. Before he had cleared leather I had my gun out and I shot the gun out of Carson's hand. "Drop the belt and get out of town," I demanded in a stern voice. Carson dropped his gun belt and lit a shuck out of town, but before he left he swore he'd get even with me, saying, "I'll get some of my brothers and come hunting you and we won't stop until you're dead!" Now, I have a lot of brothers too and they are all skilled with any type of weapon, so I wasn't particularly scared.

A couple months later when I was in Santa Fe I saw the Carsons. There were seven of them and they were hunting me. Now a body doesn't purposely jump into a fight that he knows he can't win, so I got out of there in a hurry and headed for the hills. My family had been living off the land for nigh onto two hundred years and I'd lived in the hills since I was three. I headed south into the Rockies where I figured to loose myself for a while.

On a previous visit I had found a cave in which I could hole up for a while. I stayed there for many a day catching fish from a stream and shooting deer, small game, and once in a while a buffalo for food. A few days after my arrival I was setting some snares when I stumbled upon some gold nuggets. After a careful search I found what appeared to be an abandoned gold mine. I explored further into it and found that it was indeed a gold mine and it still had a large supply of gold inside. I could only guess why it had been abandoned. Using some tools that I had found on the floor of the mine I worked for days to get that gold out and when I was done I had me a goodly sum of approximately forty-five thousand dollars. There wasn't any way I would be able to get that gold out in one trip, so I packed what I could fit on my horse in my saddle bags and hid the rest in a hole in the back of my cave.

I headed northwest to Albuquerque where I could get a fair price for my gold. I must have looked a mess since I had been in the mountains for about two years. I went down to the bank and sold my gold for twenty-five thousand dollars, a goodly sum. Then I went to the saloon for a drink, something I hadn't had for a long time. Just guess whom I met there but Jesse Carson and his seven brothers. I stepped up to the bar and ordered a drink and when I had finished my drink I got up and left. Those Carson boys were right behind me. I high-tailed it out of there and tried to lose them in all the buildings, but they were catching up. I ran down an alley and ground to a halt, for right in front of me were three of the Carson boys and four of them were on my tail. I was cornered and there wasn't anyway I could get out. The Carson boys had me surrounded and were closing in. I had my six-shooter and my Winchester ready; they wouldn't get me without a fight.

I might have been able to get two or three shots off before I was pumped full of lead. I acted those shots in my mind. I had to shoot Jesse first, then the two next to him. It would not be easy. All of a sudden shots broke out on the roof above. One man went down and then another. The Carson's started to fire back; it was time to act. I aimed my six-shooter at Jesse and squeezed off a shot. I shot two quick shots at two others and raced down the alley. Someone shot after me and I got hit in the shoulder, I fell on the ground, hit my head and passed out.

The next day I woke up in a bed with two of my brothers, Orlando and Angus, sitting by me. I tried to sit up but when I did my shoulder screamed out in pain. "Was that you two on the roof yesterday?" I asked. "Yeah, we were both up there," replied Orlando. "How did you guys happen to be there, you saved my

135

bacon!?!" I inquired. "Ma got worried when she heard the Carsons were coming after you so she sent us to find you and help you out of this mess," said Angus. "We aren't finished yet either, four of them escaped, but two of them are wounded!" "Was Jesse among the dead?" I asked. "Yeah him and his brothers Jack and Bud." said Angus. "But the others got away." "That's all right, I've still got my money with me and gold hidden up in the hills," said I. "What gold?" they shouted in unison. "The gold that I took out of an abandoned mine I found in the Rocky Mountains and I still have half of it up in them there mountains." I told them. "We will help you go up and get the rest of the gold out of there when you're better." They replied. "It's a deal," was all that I could say.

I stayed there for about three weeks. When I was almost fully healed I went into town to buy me an outfit. I already had a horse, saddle, saddlebags, my six-shooter, and my Winchester. In town I bought some ammunition for my guns, a packhorse, an extra saddle horse, some grub, and a few other odds and ends. I had myself a good outfit.

A few days later my brothers and I set out to get my gold. Each of us had two saddle horses, a Winchester, a six-shooter, and grub that could last for a month if need be. We followed the Rio Grande south to where it meets up with the Rio Puerco. From there we turned East and headed deep into the heart of the Rockies. It was an uneventful trip to my cave. I had to scout around awhile to find it, but I finally did. When I went to dig up the gold I was astounded at what I saw, where the gold should be there was just dirt! My brothers and I dug up the whole cave, but no gold was found! Where had it gone? Had someone stolen it? We searched around outside and sure enough we found a print. It was a print of a horse carrying a heavy pack. We searched further and found some more hoof prints leading north, and ever so often there were scuffmarks from a person kneeling as if they were searching for a trail or something they had dropped.

We followed the trail north until it came to a stop at the door of a small cabin with a couple of horses picketed to the ground outside. There was one window in the cabin so I decided to take a look. I peeked in the window and at a table sat the four Carson boys and two tough looking brutes, and in the center of the table was my gold. We just had to get that gold! The trouble was there were six of them and only three of us, so I went to thinking. If we could distract them somehow and get them out of the house one of us might be able to sneak in and get my gold. Their cabin was surrounded by tall grass and I thought that if we could start a fire it would get them out of the house. Once they were out we could run into the house and get my gold.

Orlando then set out to light the grass afire, while Angus held the horses, and I set to get the gold. The fire was blazing pretty well by that time. A minute or two later all six men ran out of the house in wonderment. Two of them went inside and then rushed back out with six buckets. They handed them out and dashed to the well to get water to prevent the fire from spreading. This was my chance; I darted into the house and grabbed the gold. Then I hurried back outside to the horses where Angus and Orlando were waiting. We jumped on and lit a shuck out of there. Those

Carsons and their men saw us and shot after us to no avail. They would have trailed us, but their hands were full with the fire.

From there we headed East to Dallas, Texas where a few of our brothers had a ranch, the Triple J. We stopped in Abilene to cash in our gold; we got twenty-five thousand dollars for it. We got to Dallas a few days after our stop in Abilene. Our brothers Mack, Joe and Hank were waiting for us at their ranch. When we got there supper was on the table and we were almighty hungry so we settled down to eat. Now my brothers and I could put grub away as if we hadn't eaten for months, Orlando most of all. Now the six of us cleared the table of food in about twenty minutes, man were we hungry. After supper we went to sleep in the first beds that we had slept in for months.

The next morning we awoke at the stroke of dawn. The breakfast was one of the best we'd had in a long time. All that day we helped out around the ranch. We got quite a bit done in those days. We fixed fences, roped cattle and the like.

About the time we arrived there had been a fight in town between Jobe Carson and Jose Frito in which Carson was killed and now the Carsons were hunting Frito. A couple days later Frito rode up to the ranch looking for a job. Since the Carsons were hunting him and me both, my brothers hired him. He was a good hand at roping cattle and an even better one with a gun.

The cattle were getting fat by that time and Mack, Joe, and Hank had decided to drive the cattle up to Kansas City were they had a friend who could get them the best price a head. Now we'd all go on the cattle drive, leaving a few trusted hands to watch over the ranch. A couple days later we headed out at the break of dawn and we had a hard time of it. Those cattle just didn't seem to want to go, but with the help of an old brindle steer in the lead, we somehow managed to get them going. They mostly stayed on the trail but once in a while a few would wander off and we had to get them back to the herd. It took a couple days but we finally got them trail broke. By day we drove the cattle, getting somewhere from fifteen to twenty miles a day, and by night we would set around the camp fire yarning while a few of us were out with the cattle. Around a campfire people tell stories and we got to know each other a bit more because of it.

On the third day of the drive some riders came up to camp with news for us, especially Frito and I. They told us that the Carsons were gathering up and they planned to stampede the herd and kill us all. A few days later, just after we got the heard moving, there were a bunch of gunshots, yells, and war whoops coming from just behind the herd. Those cattle were scared enough that they ran so hard they almost flew. Frito and I were on one side of the herd with Angus and Joe on the other. Between the four of us we somehow managed to contain the herd until they got to the Washita River, where they stopped to rest and drink. Luckily no one was in the front of the herd so no one got hurt.

Frito and Angus went back to camp to see how the others had fared. A while later the whole gang came down to our new camp on the Washita River. Trailing them were all the Carson boys numbering about twenty. We would have to fight it out on the banks of the Washita, and we could be sure some men would die.

We got as far away from the cattle as we could since we didn't want any of them to get shot. Those Carsons came charging at us like there was no tomorrow. We fought and fought with bullets flying all around us. All day we held our ground. By midday we were all dead beat, some of us were wounded, and a few men on both sides died. When dusk fell Orville Carson and the few of his remaining brothers held up a white flag signifying peace. We met them half way in between their side and ours. We took their guns and sent them packing down the road, we never saw them again in our born days. We had lost ten of our nineteen men. Joe, Hank, Mack, Angus, Orlando, Jose Frito, two hired hands Jake Burns and Tex Herring, and I were all that were left of us.

THE END

Printed in Great Britain
by Amazon

45107339R00085